W9-BRF-090

Savannah Spectator

Blind Item

With all the recent election excitement, Savannah has been the hub of countless celebrations, balls, galas and fund-raisers. Now that the election is over and our new senator is settling in, this reporter fears Savannah's days of excitement are over. All the recent family scandals have been grounded and after a flurry of weddings, there has been nary a socialite or a fashion *faux pas* on which to report. Will our new senator give us something juicy to read about? Perhaps a new love interest? After all, a man as scrumptious as that should only be single for so long—and it has been sooo looong....

But that is just an old reporter's wishful thinking. To be quite honest, everything has been coming up roses for our socially prominent, wealthy as sin, handsome as the devil new senator. Why, the only thing that could make his family's happiness complete is finding his niece, that poor unfortunate girl who has been missing all this time. Will she ever turn up? Stay tuned, for Savannah is always a city of surprises....

Dear Reader,

As expected, Silhouette Desire has loads of passionate, powerful and provocative love stories for you this month. Our DYNASTIES: THE DANFORTHS continuity is winding to a close with the penultimate title, *Terms of Surrender,* by Shirley Rogers. A long-lost Danforth heir may just have been found—and heavens, is this prominent family in for a big surprise! And talk about steamy secrets, Peggy Moreland is back with *Sins of a Tanner,* a stellar finale to her series THE TANNERS OF TEXAS.

If it's scandalous behavior you're looking for, look no farther than *For Services Rendered* by Anne Marie Winston. This MANTALK book—the series that offers stories strictly from the hero's point of view—has a fabulous hero who does the heroine a very special favor. Hmmmm. And Alexandra Sellers is back in Desire with a fresh installment of her SONS OF THE DESERT series. *Sheikh's Castaway* will give you plenty of sweet (and naughty) dreams.

Even more shocking situations pop up in Linda Conrad's sensual *Between Strangers.* Imagine if you were stuck on the side of the road during a blizzard and a sexy cowboy offered *you* shelter from the storm…. (Hello, are you still with me?) Rounding out the month is Margaret Allison's *Principles and Pleasures,* a daring romp between a workaholic heroine and a man she doesn't know is actually her archenemy.

So settle in for some sensual, scandalous love stories…and enjoy every moment!

Melissa Jeglinski

Melissa Jeglinski
Senior Editor, Silhouette Desire

Please address questions and book requests to:
Silhouette Reader Service
U.S.: 3010 Walden Ave., P.O. Box 1325, Buffalo, NY 14269
Canadian: P.O. Box 609, Fort Erie, Ont. L2A 5X3

TERMS OF SURRENDER
SHIRLEY ROGERS

Published by Silhouette Books
America's Publisher of Contemporary Romance

Special thanks and acknowledgment are given
to Shirley Rogers for her contribution to the
DYNASTIES: THE DANFORTHS series.

To my husband, Roger.

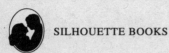 **SILHOUETTE BOOKS**

ISBN 0-373-76615-7

TERMS OF SURRENDER

SHIRLEY ROGERS

lives in Virginia with her husband, two cats and an adorable Maltese named Blanca. She has two grown children, a son and a daughter. As a child, she was known for having a vivid imagination. It wasn't until she started reading romances that she realized her true destiny was writing them! Besides reading, she enjoys traveling, seeing movies and spending time with her family.

DYNASTIES: THE DANFORTHS

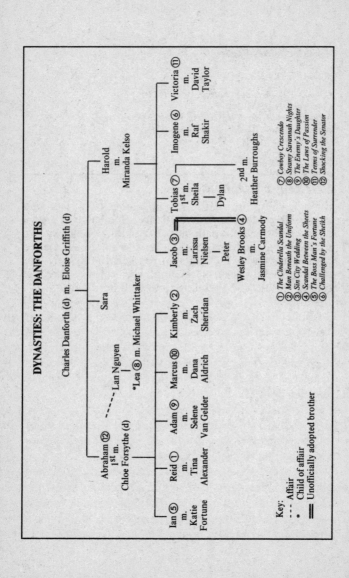

Charles Danforth (d) m. Eloise Griffith (d)

Sara

Harold
m.
Miranda Kelso

Abraham ⑫
1st m.
Chloe Forsythe (d)

- - - Lan Nguyen

*Lea ⑧ m. Michael Whittaker

Reid ① | Kimberly ② | Jacob ③ | Tobias ⑦ | Imogene ⑥ | Victoria ⑪
m. | m. | m. | 1st m. | m. | m.
Tina | Zach | Larissa | Sheila | Raf | David
Alexander | Sheridan | Nielsen | | Shakir | Taylor

Ian ⑤ | Adam ⑨ | Marcus ⑩
m. | m. | m.
Katie | Selene | Dana
Fortune | Van Gelder | Aldrich

Peter

Dylan

Wesley Brooks ④
m.
Jasmine Carmody

2nd m.
Heather Burroughs

① *The Cinderella Scandal*
② *Man Beneath the Uniform*
③ *Sin City Wedding*
④ *Scandal Between the Sheets*
⑤ *The Boss Man's Fortune*
⑥ *Challenged by the Sheikh*

⑦ *Cowboy Crescendo*
⑧ *Steamy Savannah Nights*
⑨ *The Enemy's Daughter*
⑩ *The Laws of Passion*
⑪ *Terms of Surrender*
⑫ *Shacking the Senator*

Key:
- - - Affair
* Child of affair
═══ Unofficially adopted brother

One

"Promise me."

Believing he'd misheard his dying father's whispered words, David Taylor knelt beside the massive oak bed and leaned closer. "Promise you what?" he asked softly. Considering their estranged relationship, he wondered what could be so important that his father would ask *anything* of him.

"Promise me you'll take care of Tanya."

That he hadn't expected. Of all the possibilities of what Edward Taylor would ask, David would never have thought of Tanya Winters.

Drawing in a deep breath, he looked into fatigued blue eyes. The figure lying before him no longer seemed the father who had been so strict and difficult through most of David's life. Now he saw him as a man, a shadow of the forceful figure he'd seen through the eyes of a child. At sixty, his hair, once light brown, had turned nearly white. Rapid loss of weight had left his skin wrinkled and pasty. Cancer had taken him down quickly.

"Father, I—"

"Promise!" Edward gasped for breath as he made a feeble effort to grab his son's arm.

"I promise," David said quickly, knowing there was little else he could do to ease his father's mind in his last moments. "Easy, now." He tightened his hand on his father's and encouraged him to lie back, wincing at the inflection of pain in the older man's eyes. "I'll take care of her. You have my word."

It wasn't an easy promise to make, David thought, as Edward succumbed to the weakness of his body and eased back to rest on the mattress. Since arriving at Cottonwood Plantation in Georgia, David had seen Tanya Winters, his father's employee, only a few minutes. But that had been long enough to stir up old, unwanted memories of his own deep-seated awareness of her—an awareness that hadn't dissipated in the five years he'd been away.

And from the way she'd greeted him with barely restrained disdain, she hadn't forgotten their heated parting. But there would be time to deal with Tanya later. Right now, his father was all that mattered.

He looked at his father's still body, his closed eyes. David almost hadn't made it back in time. His father's personal physician, Mason Brewer, standing only a few feet away, had informed him it wasn't likely Edward would make it through the day. David swallowed past the knot in his throat. He still couldn't believe his father was dying.

"We'd better get Tanya," Dr. Brewer stated in a quiet voice.

Their eyes met. David nodded and stood. He'd spent less than thirty private minutes with his father, and he supposed that at some point during that time, the two of them had made a peace of sorts. They'd never gotten along, and now they would never have the chance to make things totally right between them.

David's mother, Eloise, had died when he was ten, and after the loss of his wife, Edward had never been the same. As a child, David had tried to please his father. As a teenager, he'd given up trying when nothing he'd said or done seemed to bridge the gap between them. After graduating college, he'd moved away. His decision not to stay and help run his father's peanut plantation had widened an already emotional chasm between them.

So he'd left the plantation just outside of Cotton Creek, a rural town an hour's distance from Savannah, determined to make his own way in life. And he'd done well. His Atlanta-based acquisitions and mergers company, Taylor Corp., had made him successful and affluent. But it seemed that even that hadn't been enough to gain his father's approval.

The door opened and he looked over to see Tanya Winters enter the room. His gaze followed her movements as she slowly walked across the floor, her body fluid and graceful. As a seventeen-year-old, she'd been cute; as a woman, well, stunning was the only way to describe her.

But despite her slim, athletic body, she seemed to be barely holding up under the strain of Edward's illness. She'd pulled her straight, amber-blond hair into a ponytail at the nape of her neck, baring absolutely flawless skin. Her amber-gold eyes, swollen and red from crying, were filled with sadness.

As David stepped aside, she glanced at him, then just as easily dismissed him, giving her complete attention to his father. Though her movements seemed effortless, he sensed the energy it took to gather herself together and approach the bed.

She sat beside his father and leaned close to him. "I'm here, Edward," she whispered, her voice trembling. Slim fingers lifted his father's wrinkled hand and held it as she stroked his forehead with her other hand.

She spoke close to his ear, and he saw the old man's craggy face change, his eyes momentarily brighten. A weak smile formed on his dry lips. David's awareness of Tanya warred with jealousy and resentment. He hadn't expected to feel anything for her, but the minute she'd greeted him at the door, he'd realized that leaving hadn't done a thing to get her out of his system.

From her cool looks, apparently she hadn't forgiven his transgressions that last day he'd been at Cottonwood, when he'd dragged her in his arms and kissed her before walking out the door. While David felt like an outsider in his family home, she appeared at ease, as if she had more right to be there than he did.

She'd come to live at Cottonwood as an intern through a program designed to help underprivileged youth. His father had taken an immediate liking to the young waif. By the looks of things, their relationship had grown deeper— they'd formed a stronger bond than David had ever shared with his father. He turned away to give them privacy.

Hearing a sharp gasp, he turned back and looked, his eyes immediately focusing on her. In what seemed like slow-motion, Dr. Brewer rushed over and withdrew his stethoscope. Tanya slumped on the bedside. As if it were perfectly natural, as if he hadn't been away for years, David went to her. Sliding his arm around her shoulders, he drew her away. Despite her disdain for him, she'd cared deeply for his father.

David's gaze found the doctor's, and he quietly confirmed the worst. His father was gone.

On a soft cry, Tanya turned into David's embrace and buried her head against his shoulder. His heart heavy, David nodded to Dr. Brewer. He started to lead Tanya from the room, but she stiffened and tried to pull free. "You can't do anything for him now, Tanya," he said gently. "Come on."

Shaking with grief and despair, Tanya Winters broke down in tears as David led her out of the bedroom, down the stairs and into the sitting room. Bright sunlight shone through massive windows, an almost painful contrast to the emptiness she felt inside. The only person on earth she cared about was gone. What was she going to do without him?

A fresh wave of anguish overcame her. Hot tears streamed down her cheeks, robbing her of strength, and she clung to David for support. He held her tightly, keeping her from crumbling, whispering that everything would be all right.

Oh, she wanted so much to believe it would be. But it wasn't possible, was it? The man who'd given her a chance when no one else would help her was gone. She'd come a long way from the homeless teenager that Edward Taylor had taken in five years ago. Standing in the huge, immaculate room, she looked around, searching for solace in the familiar surroundings. The floral print settee. The massive, hand-carved mantel over the fireplace. This magnificent plantation in Georgia was the only place she had to call home.

Her life before moving here remained a mystery to her. She still didn't remember how, at seventeen, she'd ended up lying unconscious on a rural road with a concussion, which had left her with retrograde amnesia. All she really knew was what the hospital staff had said her identification provided—that she was Tanya Winters, a streetwise kid who had no family to claim her. By a stroke of luck, Edward Taylor had heard of her plight and had offered her a second chance and an opportunity to work on his peanut farm.

She'd learned so much from him, had worked alongside him, devouring his attention and knowledge. With stiff competition from other farmers, it had become increasingly difficult to continue making a reasonable profit selling peanuts. At her urging, he'd changed their major crop from peanuts to soybeans. Tanya had researched the growing soybean industry, and she'd provided Edward with a plethora of information with which to make an informed decision. The farm was currently turning a larger profit than it had in years.

Oh, God, what would become of her now? She loved this house and the land and the people who worked here. She loved the small, quaint town of Cotton Creek, where everyone accepted her for who she was. They didn't care that she came from poor beginnings. Now that his father was gone, would David let her stay and continue managing Cottonwood?

As if that was going to happen. After their hurtful parting years ago, she was amazed that he was even offering her the comfort of his arms. The summer she'd arrived, he'd returned from college, and though she'd harbored a crush on him, he'd barely tolerated her.

David had fought with his father over nearly everything, and at the end of the summer, announced he was leaving. Wanting him to stay, she'd made a fool of herself and had thrown herself at him. He'd kissed her senseless, then had thrust her away from him and stormed out.

His rejection had been devastating.

But she was no longer that shy, wayward teen. Edward had molded her, had taught her to be proud of who she was. And now, more than ever, she had to be strong.

Her tears began to subside. Aware that David was still holding her, she raised her head and met his gaze. "I'm sorry." Disturbed by the flare of awareness at his nearness, Tanya moved out of his embrace, not wanting him to know that she still cared, that he could still make her feel. It was the grief, she rationalized. Her emotions were just out of whack.

She sniffed and met his gaze again. His piercing blue eyes studied her, and in that moment, the shock of realizing she was still attracted to him was nothing compared to her growing anger. Though she knew that father and son hadn't gotten along well, she was disappointed that he hadn't returned home immediately when he'd learned of his father's illness. "What happened, David?" she demanded, pausing before one of the long, narrow windows in the room. "Why did it take you so long to get home?"

"When you called, I was out of the country." His lips twisted briefly. "I ran into some unexpected delays because of bad weather on the west coast. I got here as soon as I could."

She stared at him, her gaze hard and unrelenting. "Your father became seriously ill two months ago."

"What?"

Tanya searched his expression, then she realized that she'd truly caught him off-guard. "You didn't know?"

"I had no idea."

"But he told me that he'd called you," she insisted. "I asked him several times to try to make amends with you."

"Hell would have frozen over before he would have admitted needing my help." David shoved his hands in his pockets. "We talked briefly a couple of months ago, but he never mentioned that he was sick. I haven't heard from him since." Though Tanya seemed surprised that his father hadn't confided in him about his illness, David wasn't. Until the very end, their relationship had been strained.

She drew in a breath, then nodded. "He said he had called you, but he never told me what the two of you had discussed. I'd assumed he'd informed you that his health was declining. I asked if you were coming home. Your father said no." Her gaze held his. "I thought it was because you didn't care about him."

"I didn't know he was sick," he assured her. "The first I heard of him being so ill was when I received your message two days ago. I'd have come back sooner if I'd known."

"Really?" Tanya wanted to believe him, wanted to believe he wasn't the callous, selfish person she thought him to be. But his absence the past five years told another story. If he'd cared about his father, he would have tried harder to understand him.

"I guess there are funeral arrangements that need to be made," David said, changing the subject. He didn't want to discuss his feelings for his father. Not with Tanya.

Tears filled her eyes, then spilled down her cheeks.

She brushed them away with her fingers. "No. Edward had talked with his lawyer and everything has been taken care of. I tried to help him, but he insisted that I had enough to do managing the plantation."

"Managing the plantation?" David stared at her in disbelief. "*You're* the manager?" he asked, his tone incredulous.

Tanya lifted her chin. "Yes." He approached her, stopping only a few feet away, his questioning gaze fueling her irritation.

"You're way too young and inexperienced to be handling this entire plantation."

"Too young?" she repeated, clearly insulted. "Who do you think has been taking care of everything since your father became ill?"

"I'm sure you've been doing the best you could for the past couple of months, but I find it difficult to believe that you can handle this place on your own."

Tanya couldn't believe his arrogance. "Actually, due to your father's worsening condition, I've been running the farm for quite a while. Besides handling the daily operations, I've installed a computer system, bringing the office and the accounting procedures into the twenty-first century. I also take care of this house and supervise the entire staff." Five people shared the duties of the household and grounds. Edward had taken great pride in his ancestral home.

"You've made yourself right at home, haven't you?" David's quiet voice was coated with a tinge of accusation. If the old man had put the entire plantation in Tanya's immature hands, maybe his father's illness had gone to his mind. Then another thought hit him. Maybe

Tanya had manipulated his father in order to inherit his fortune. She'd arrived a streetwise teen, far from innocent. Living at Cottonwood with servants at her beck and call wasn't something she'd want to give up. And because he'd been away for years, she would have had plenty of time to work her name into his father's will.

David shouldn't care. But this was about more than just money. He knew what it was like to be burned by a woman. He'd broken up with his ex-fiancé, Melanie, when he'd figured out that she'd only been interested in him because of his wealth. Thank God he'd come to his senses and had seen her for the gold digger that she was before he'd walked down the aisle.

And he'd be damned if he'd stand by and see everything his father worked for put in Tanya Winters's name.

"Made myself at home? What do you mean by that?" Tanya felt as if she'd been slapped.

Jealousy got the best of David. That, in addition to fighting his own awareness of her, egged him on to find out exactly what kind of relationship she'd had with his father. "What else have you been doing for my father?" He looked at her mouth, could still remember the effect she had on him when he'd kissed her. And how hard it had been to walk away from her and the plantation.

"That's insulting to me and offensive to your father's memory," Tanya grated through clenched teeth. "Your father—" she began, then had to stop when her voice broke. She took a breath, then tried again. "Your father was very kind to me. He gave me a home, a place to belong."

The churning in David's gut subsided. That Tanya hadn't had an intimate relationship with his father pleased him more than it should have. "I was out of line. I'm sorry."

"Thank you for that." But she didn't sound appeased.

He raised a brow. "Your memory hasn't returned?"

She shook her head, sadness filling her. God, she wished it had. Still, she didn't admit to him that lately she'd been experiencing odd sensations, a strange perception of…something. Tanya wasn't convinced that the odd happenings weren't just her imagination. Not wanting to trouble Edward, she hadn't even told him, nor had she mentioned the intense, disturbing dreams she'd started having over the past month. "I still don't remember anything before waking up in the hospital."

Still too vivid was the fear that smothered her when she had awakened in strange surroundings. She hadn't known a soul. And, oh God, the panic when she'd realized that she hadn't even known her own name. According to the police, she had been a street kid with an impressive juvenile record who was scheduled to move into a group home. Offering her a chance to turn her life around, Edward had saved her from that horrible experience.

"So you stayed on at Cottonwood out of gratitude?"

"In the beginning." It had been fear, mostly. Because there had been nothing else for her. She'd needed something, *someone* to cling to.

"Ah, I see."

"Do you?" There was doubt in his eyes. He'd been away for years. She dismissed his attitude as ignorance. "I've handled the daily operations of the plantation for almost a year. Though at the time Edward didn't know he was ill, he'd begun to slow down. Your father relied on me to keep things going."

He studied her for a long moment. "There's a lot more to running this plantation besides growing peanuts."

He doesn't know, her mind whispered. *He has no idea that the plantation no longer produces peanuts.* Tanya opened her mouth to tell him, then stopped herself, deciding to wait to drop that news on him.

"I know that." She straightened her shoulders. Well over six feet, he towered over her five-foot-six-inch frame, but she refused to be intimidated by him. "I've computerized the schedule of crop rotation for the next five years." Along with changing the main crop to soybeans, the plantation grew cotton. Rotation of crops was important to fight disease and insure a successful harvest year after year. "And I personally negotiated a health insurance plan for your father's permanent employees. I haven't exactly been living off of your father."

"I didn't mean to imply that you don't work."

"Yes, you did."

She had him there, David thought. Apparently Tanya was in more control of the plantation than he'd realized. It was going to make it that much tougher to tell her that she was out of a job.

"Look. I really don't want to argue with you. I'll take your word that you've been running things as well as you could." David hadn't seen the accounts, so he wasn't about to compliment her on her success.

Her face softened. "I did it because I loved him."

"He cared for you, as well." David watched her thoughtfully. "His last words to me were about you."

"They were?" Surprise widened her expressive eyes. That his father had spoken of her warmed her heart. "What did he say?"

For a moment he remained silent, almost as if he'd rather not reveal their conversation. "He made me promise to take care of you."

"What?" Stunned, she stared at him. David taking care of her. What a laugh. He didn't even like her.

"I promised him I would." He hesitated, then went on, "So, I don't want you to think that I'm going to just turn you out with nowhere to go. I've been thinking that since you never had the opportunity, it might be a good idea for you to go to college. I'll provide you with an expense account."

It took a moment for Tanya to absorb his words. When she did, her heart began to pound. "College?" Seconds later, her surprise gave way to anger. "I can't believe you. Your father isn't even cold in his grave and you're throwing me out?"

David shook his head. "I'm not throwing—"

"You heartless bastard. Now I know exactly why you and your father didn't get along."

Anger flashed in his eyes. "You don't know anything about me."

"I know you broke his heart when you left." She snatched a photo of David when he'd graduated from college off a nearby table. "I know that some days he sat in this very room and stared at your picture. I know that rarely a week went by that he didn't mention you in some way." Replacing the picture, she confronted him. "And now I know just how coldhearted you are."

Tanya started around him, then stopped. "Let me ask you something, David. In all honesty, what do you know about this plantation? You haven't been back for years. For that matter, what do you know about growing soybeans?" Her eyes stayed on his, watching his expression change to confusion.

"Soybeans?"

"Yes, soybeans. Your father changed the main crop from peanuts to soybeans several years ago." She gave a bitter laugh. "You didn't know? Well, of course not. Because you didn't care enough about this plantation to keep up with the changes. I know a lot more about this farm than you do."

As much as David hated to admit it, she was right. He hadn't been back since the summer he'd graduated from college. He'd barely stayed in touch by telephone. "Why did my father stop growing peanuts?" Unable to believe what she was saying, he looked out the window as if he could tell with a glance that she was speaking the truth.

"What difference does that make? Right now you need me."

David gave his head a shake, trying to make sense of what she'd said. "All right, if what you say is true, I'll admit you have a point." But that didn't mean he trusted her. "We'll try this on a trial basis. You stay for, say, three months. If you can't run the place, you'll agree I'm right and leave. At that time, my offer to send you to college will still stand." It seemed like the perfect solution. No matter what she said, there was no way that Tanya could run this place.

Tanya's gaze never left his. If he thought she was going to fail, he'd be sadly mistaken. "I'll take you up on that." With that, she turned to walk away, but was drawn up short when David's hand clamped around her arm. "Take your hand off me."

He complied immediately. "We're not finished."

"For now, we are. If you don't mind, I've had all I can take of you today." She continued to the door and yanked it open.

"Tanya—" he called, but she stormed out. The door slammed behind her.

Well, great. Now look what you've done.

And soybeans? What was *that* about? Why had his father changed from peanuts, a crop he'd grown all of his life, to soybeans? It didn't make sense.

David walked over and poured himself a bourbon. He stared at the amber liquid, then threw it down his throat, savoring the burn. Maybe he *was* a bastard. He hadn't meant to make Tanya feel as if she had to leave Cottonwood immediately. The strange thing was, a foolish part of him wanted her to stay. But if she stayed, David knew she'd get under his skin.

For the sake of his heart, he could never let that happen.

A cold chill swept over her, but Tanya knew it had nothing to do with the temperature of the November morning. Out of the corner of her eye she watched David, who sat across the room. His father's attorney was seated behind the large, antique desk across from them in Edward's study. He'd only been gone a few days, and here they were, waiting for the reading of his will.

Oh, how she missed him. Tears formed in her eyes as she thought of never seeing Edward again. Fear gripped her. Once again, she was all alone in the world.

Though David had remained at the plantation, she'd managed to avoid being alone with him. Their earlier confrontation had cemented her opinion that he had been cold and unfeeling when it came to his father. As for his opinion of her, he'd pretty much made it clear that he didn't want her at Cottonwood. To his credit, he had tried to apologize, but nothing he said could have erased his hurtful words.

"If I could have your attention," Clifford Danson said as he looked up from the papers in his hand. He waited until both David and Tanya met his gaze. "David, your father asked that you both be present because the terms of the will affect each of you."

Uneasy, Tanya glanced at David. She hadn't expected to be mentioned in the will. Her eyes began to sting with fresh tears.

"As his only son, you stand to inherit this entire estate," the lawyer continued. "I'm aware that the two of you didn't get along, but your father believed that Cottonwood is your birthright. He felt deeply that you should receive it."

David nodded. If he was surprised or pleased, he didn't show it. He should be happy, Tanya thought. He was getting what he wanted. She was the one who was going to have to leave.

Mr. Danson looked at Tanya. "He cared very deeply for you, as well, young lady."

Trying not to cry, Tanya blinked. "I know, but I don't understand why I'm even here." She didn't look at David. She couldn't, not without feeling a rush of resentment and disappointment in him. And in spite of that, she had to deal with her damned attraction to him. It was insulting just to think about.

"I'm getting to that," the lawyer promised. "As I

said, David, you stand to inherit the entire estate. However, there's a stipulation that involves Miss Winters." He glanced from one to the other, his face somber as his gaze paused on David. "Keep in mind that these were his wishes, and he was very specific about them. In order to inherit Cottonwood Plantation, you must live here—"

"What?" David came to his feet.

Danson held up his hand, staving further comment. "There's more. He's also stipulated that, in addition, Miss Winters is to be kept on as the manager for as long as she desires."

Two

"This is ridiculous! Hell, it's not even feasible!" David slammed his hands flat on his father's desk, confronting Clifford Danson. He couldn't believe what he was hearing. "I have a business in Atlanta to run. My life is there. I *can't* live here."

The lawyer lowered his reading glasses to the edge of his nose as he shook his head, the look in his eyes indicating that he understood the dilemma but was powerless to help solve it. "I'm sorry," he apologized, as if the situation were somehow his fault. "The terms of the will are spelled out in very specific language. In order to receive your inheritance, you must live here. That's not negotiable."

Straightening, David looked around, then again leveled his gaze on the older man. "How long?"

"For the term of one full year."

"A year," he repeated with disgust. His hands went to his hips. "And if I don't agree to these ludicrous terms?"

"You'll forfeit everything."

The room fell into deafening silence. David's attention shifted to Tanya. Every nerve ending in his body came alive as he looked at her. Her eyes were wide with what he construed to be shock, her lips nearly white. The reading of the will had staggered her, as well.

Or had it? his mind taunted. Had Tanya been manipulating Edward, waiting for his demise, so she could benefit from his illness? Though his body seemed to respond to her on a million levels, he didn't really know her, did he? Was she capable of such deceit? When he'd pressed her about her relationship with his father, she'd unequivocally denied anything intimate. But that didn't mean that she wasn't after his father's money.

More determined than ever to find out, he turned his attention back to the lawyer. "If I don't accept these terms, what happens to Cottonwood?"

Danson cleared his throat. He picked up the will and flipped a few pages. "Pursuant to the terms of the will," he began reading verbatim from the document, "the aforementioned—"

"Skip the jargon and get to the point," David demanded.

"All right." The lawyer dropped the papers to the desk. "In the event that you decide not to make Cottonwood your permanent home for one year, Miss Winters will inherit the entire estate."

"What?" Tanya gasped. David whirled to face her, his expression furious. "I had no idea that Edward had done this," Tanya blurted out, floored by the terms of the will. David was staring at her as if she were the devil.

And why not? What had Edward been thinking when he'd instructed his lawyer to make such a crazy stipulation? "I love my job and I want to continue working here, but the plantation belongs to you. No matter what's written in the will."

"Now if Tanya decides to leave on her own accord, you'll inherit free and clear." The lawyer gathered the legal documents in front of him, stuffed them into his briefcase, then stood and walked around the desk. "That's pretty much the extent of the terms. I've left a copy of the will for you to read." He shook hands with David.

Turning to Tanya, his expression gentled as he took her hand in his and held it a moment before letting go. "Let me know if I can do anything for you. Edward was very insistent that he didn't want you to worry about anything. Please contact me when you've made your decisions. I'll see myself out."

Tanya watched the lawyer leave, then flinched when she met David's hard stare. She could imagine how he felt, and despite the fact that he didn't seem to trust her, her heart went out to him. Edward had put them both in quite a predicament. "David, I'm telling you the truth. I didn't know a thing about your father's intentions."

"Really?" he asked, a hard edge to his voice.

His scathing look sent a chill down her spine. "I swear I didn't." Hurt radiated through her entire body. That he thought her capable of… She couldn't even finish the thought.

Her heart pounding, she got to her feet, then realized too late that she was shaking so hard, she could barely hold her own weight. Leaning against the chair for support, she faced him.

"I guess the old man got the last laugh, after all,

didn't he?" David shook his head. He'd been delusional to believe that he had made any kind of peace with his father. If he accepted the terms of the will, he'd be strapped to the plantation, unable to return to Atlanta.

"I don't think Edward was purposefully trying to hurt you," she answered, not really understanding his comment. It was difficult for her to believe that the man she knew and loved had inflicted the pain in David's eyes.

"You don't know what you're talking about."

She groped for an explanation. "There were days he wasn't thinking clearly. Maybe he wasn't in his right mind when he made those stipulations."

"If that were the case, Danson would have never had the document drawn up." Clifford Danson had been his father's lawyer for many years. David was sure the man wouldn't have done anything he deemed unethical, not even for a longtime friend.

"Still, your father must have believed he was looking out for your best interest."

"It seems to me that he had *your* best interest in mind," he grated.

"I know it looks like that, but—"

"Looks like it?" His shoulders visibly tightened. "At the very least, you have a job until you no longer want it." There went his plans for sending her away. Which was going to play hell with his libido. He didn't need Tanya around, didn't want to be reminded of his attraction to her.

Or allow it room to grow.

Tanya tilted her head, lifting her chin a notch. "I'm not going to pretend that I'm not relieved I have a job and a place to live," she admitted, remembering his plans to send her away. Maybe that's what Edward had been afraid of, that David wouldn't keep the plantation—that he'd sell it.

"Now, why doesn't that surprise me?" David suspected, now that she'd been given a choice, she wasn't ever going to leave. He had no alternative but to keep her on as the plantation manager. Which also meant that he would have to stay. The farm had permanent employees, people who depended on their jobs to make a living. It was now his responsibility to be sure they had a secure future. He didn't know what Tanya had been doing with the finances, and until he did, he wasn't prepared to trust her.

He moved closer, stopping only inches from her. "But don't think for a minute that I'm going to walk away from here and leave everything to you." The plantation was *his* heritage, not Tanya's. Maybe he hadn't been around for years. But his absence didn't mean that he didn't care about his legacy. His father was the reason he'd left. He grimaced at the irony of the situation. His father was also the reason he'd returned and was being forced to stay.

"I'm not expecting you to," she told him, her tone cool. Despite what Edward had written in his will, the plantation belonged to David, not her. She was thankful that she wasn't homeless, but she wasn't going to apologize for her close relationship with his father.

"Really?" He eyed her with speculation. "You're prepared to live here with me?"

Tanya gulped. Live there with David? That thought made all of her girlish dreams of him come back to her in a rush.

Stop it! Don't let your heart get involved. Unlike you,

he considers himself trapped. He doesn't want to live here, with or without you.

"Yes," she answered, determined to get along with him. How hard could living in the same house be, after all? It was a big house. Huge, even. They'd sleep in separate bedrooms. And once planting season arrived, with all the work to be done, they probably wouldn't even share meals. David wouldn't be there all of the time. He'd have to leave at some time or another on business, wouldn't he?

"I guess it's settled, then." David wanted to look away, but instead found his gaze sliding from her perfectly poised face to her sleek, enticing neck. Her creamy skin begged to be touched, and it was all he could do to keep his hands to himself, which brought another thought to mind.

If he and Tanya both lived at the plantation, how was he going to control his attraction to her? Hell, even after the lawyer had dropped his bombshell, even when David should have been feeling nothing but indignation and resentment, he was drawn to her.

The last thing he wanted was to become involved with Tanya. Melanie had made him wary of his judgment when it came to women. Finding out she had just been using him had been a blessing in disguise.

He'd been humiliated, played for a fool. Since his disastrous relationship with Melanie, he'd done a good job of keeping his distance from any woman who wanted more than a night or two of pleasure. There was no way he was going to let Tanya get under his skin. He'd use the time that he had to be around her to become immune to her. And when the sentence his father had imposed upon him by requiring him to live on the plantation for a year was up, he'd return to his life in Atlanta.

By then, Tanya Winters would be completely out of his system.

Though David had planned on going over the accounts of the plantation first thing the next morning, he'd received a call from his friend and vice president, Justin West, about Taylor Corp.'s latest acquisition, a Japanese computer software company. Upon hearing of his father's illness, he'd been forced to leave during final negotiations. David had made his apologies and had put Justin in charge, confident that he could close the deal.

Still, there had been a couple of key issues to discuss this morning that neither of them had anticipated, and it had taken more time than David had realized. Once he was done, he'd called Jessica, his personal assistant, and put the wheels in motion to turn his father's study into a satellite office so he would be able to handle much of his firm's business from the plantation.

Looking up from the work he'd retrieved from his briefcase, David's gaze swept his father's study, taking in his large book collection on shelving that covered one entire wall. Struck with a feeling of disorientation, he sat back and stared at the many volumes, perfectly categorized and alphabetized. And looking as if they'd never been read. As a child, he'd never been allowed to touch them.

Now they're yours.

His chest tightened a fraction as he got to his feet and walked across the room, stopping in front of the massive wall of books. Scanning the titles, his gaze stopped on an original edition of poems. He hadn't known his father had liked poetry. The sad truth was that he hadn't known his father at all.

That wasn't your fault.

Maybe it was, David thought in the still silence. Tanya certainly thought it was. If he'd been the kind of son his father had wanted, he'd have swallowed his pride and stayed on the plantation. Maybe then he would have known the man.

It wouldn't have changed anything.

Sadly, he believed that was true. When his mother was alive, they'd been like a family. David could re- member, as a boy, tossing a ball around with his father, laughing as they played.

When Eloise Taylor had died, everything had changed. David had become a detail to deal with, rather than a son to love. He hadn't understood then. He still didn't. But he'd quickly learned that his father hadn't wanted or needed his love.

Replacing the book, he glanced around. No, it wouldn't have made a difference if he'd stayed. He would have been suffocated by his father's strong will, with neither of them being happy in the end. Edward would never have allowed him to make any decisions concerning the farm or its business. When he'd returned home from college, he had approached his father about updating the plantation's equipment. Edward hadn't even given his reasons for change consideration.

Tanya, however, had been able to talk him into a lot more than changing the equipment. Hell, his father had changed his principal crop!

At the thought of Tanya, David glanced at his watch and realized he was late for his meeting with her. Leav- ing the room, he started in the direction of the storage building she'd pointed out to him after breakfast that morning.

A few minutes later, he walked into one of the large metal buildings that housed the equipment used on the plantation. "I'm sorry I'm late," he said by way of a greeting. "I got caught up in a telephone conference."

His gaze ran over her, then came back to her face. Dressed in blue jeans and a soft knit sweater to ward off the morning chill, she looked at home, right down to her worn brown work boots. With her blond hair pulled into a tight ponytail and a clipboard in her hand, she'd apparently been at work awhile.

"That's okay. I had some things to take care of while I was waiting," Tanya assured him, not really surprised. She hadn't expected him to make the plantation's operation a priority. Clearly, the business of his firm in Atlanta took precedence in his life. Well, that was okay with her. She didn't need David micromanaging every aspect of her work. Things would run more smoothly between them if he'd just let her continue to run the plantation without interference.

"It really couldn't be helped," he insisted, feeling the need to justify his tardiness. His gaze wandered down her body. Her figure had changed over the years. Though still slim, her breasts were fuller, her hips nicely rounded. He shifted his attention to her perfectly shaped oval face, her pert nose and wide amber eyes. As she walked toward him, her body moved with a grace that seemed to contradict her poor upbringing.

What was it about this woman that, after five years, he hadn't been able to get her out of his system? Apparently his father had seen something special in her, as well, or he wouldn't have asked David to take care of her. "But I'm all yours now."

All yours.

Tanya swallowed hard at the thought. Dressed in khaki-colored dress pants and a pale blue dress shirt that looked like they cost more than she'd spent on clothes in the last year, David was one very handsome man. Yet, there was little about him that reminded her of the young man she'd lost her heart to when she was seventeen.

The past five years had been more than kind to him. His shoulders and chest had filled out with well-toned muscles. His face, more chiseled and angular, made him favor his father more than she realized. He was enough to turn any woman's head twice.

But his piercing blue eyes drew her to him. There was an emptiness in them that she longed to fill, a sadness that she wanted so much to ease.

"Tanya?"

Realizing David was speaking to her, Tanya started. Getting her thoughts back on the business at hand, she said, "Um, all right. Let me show you around."

As Tanya talked, David listened attentively, and he had to admit he was impressed with her thorough knowledge of the workings of the plantation and the equipment used to run it. Apparently she'd been telling the truth when she'd said she'd been in charge for some time.

However, he was still stunned by Edward's decision to change crops. It was a decision that David just didn't understand. "What made my father decide to stop growing peanuts?" he asked as he examined the drill used to break the ground and seed it.

Biting her lip, Tanya glanced briefly at him. Knowing her answer wouldn't make things between the two of them any smoother, she had to be honest. "Several years ago, I did a study on the production of peanuts in the state of Georgia and in other states where peanuts are main crops. Production costs were on the rise, and Cottonwood's profits had begun to slip."

"That's part of the business, isn't it?" David reasoned, studying the apprehensive expression in her amber eyes, and wondering what caused it. "Supply and demand and all that."

Tanya's brows wrinkled. "That's simplifying it quite a bit," she answered, her tone taut. "The future earnings of peanuts was looking bleak. Changes in government regulations have hurt peanut farmers tremendously. Many growers have had to make adjustments in their crops and a lot of independent farmers have gone under."

"Was the plantation in danger of that?" David asked, realizing he'd inadvertently insulted her. That's what he got for letting his mind wander. If he hadn't been thinking about what was going on behind those expressive eyes, he wouldn't have said something so stupid.

Obviously, he'd been away from the agriculture industry too long. Busy running his own business, he hadn't even thought about the peanut market.

"I don't think it was that bad, but the plantation would never have been as profitable as it had in the past. Your father seemed worried. I began to research soybeans and pitched the idea of going into the soybean market to him." She gestured toward the door. "Do you want to take some time now to look over the accounts?"

David nodded casually, but inside his chest ached. His father would never have accepted such an idea from him. He reminded himself that it wasn't Tanya's fault that he'd never gotten along with his father. "Why soybeans?" he asked, opening the door for her. She walked out and he followed.

"The demand for soybeans has increased as people have become more health conscious. They're used for an array of foods, such as veggie burgers, granola bars, potato chips and even chocolate."

"Chocolate? You're kidding!"

She smiled, but the expression never reached her eyes. "They're used in many non-food products, as well," she continued as they walked the footpath to the house. "Like lipstick, plastic and paints. It just seemed like the right time to switch the farm over to a growing, marketable crop."

David still hadn't seen the accounts, so he reserved his opinion until he'd had a chance to study them. "I have to admit that I'm stunned you were able to convince my father to make such a drastic change," he stated, his eyes drawn to her face, which showed signs of strain. He knew his father's death hadn't been easy for her, but other than that one incident yesterday, she hadn't shared her feelings with him.

"At first, Edward wasn't exactly excited about the idea," she admitted, a little surprised that David actually seemed interested in what was happening on the farm. "We discussed it for months. I had to show him massive amounts of documentation, including detailed earning projections. Your father could be very stubborn."

"You're telling me." As they arrived at the back of the house, he opened the door, then followed her inside. "After college, I tried to convince him to make some changes on the farm, newly developed techniques that would have increased production, but he wouldn't listen to me." After that, David had been convinced that he and his father would never have been able to work side by side.

Tanya hadn't known that. Edward had never mentioned David's ideas concerning the farm. She wondered if he would have stayed if his father had listened to him. David's honest admission caused Tanya to stop and think. Though he spoke without emotion, she could see the sadness in his eyes. His resentment toward her was understandable. Even expected. Which was going to make working with him even more difficult.

"I remember the two of you quarreling," she admitted softly as she paused just outside the door of the study. "I'd always hoped you could mend things between you." Looking up, she met his gaze. "Despite how you got along, your father did care about you."

He didn't reply, which disheartened her. Perhaps her own grief would have been easier to handle if she could have shared her feelings with David. But she hadn't dared to talk to him after the reading of the will.

He'd been angry. She didn't blame him. Nothing she could have said would have changed the way he felt. He resented her, and he didn't want to be her friend. Despite her attraction to him, she had to accept that he was merely tolerating her presence. Not that she didn't hold her own anger toward him. His accusations of her being intimate with his father had been uncalled for. That he could even think such a thing told her how callous he'd become.

Sighing heavily, she went into the study. Nothing was the same without Edward. The next year promised to be not only physically, but mentally draining. How was she going to get through this on her own?

Tanya's steps faltered as she walked into the room. Tears crested in her eyes at the lingering scent of Edward's pipe tobacco. Oh, God. She couldn't handle this. Not now. She desperately needed to be alone. At least until she pulled herself together.

As she wavered, David came to her aid, grabbing her by the shoulders and offering her support. "Are you all right?" he asked, scrutinizing her features.

"I'm fine," she insisted. But she wasn't. Tears ran unchecked down her cheeks. She sniffed, then was mortified when even more tears followed.

"You don't look it," he replied, his tone short as he took in her ashen face. "What's wrong?" He longed to pull her against him and hold her, but considering their earlier disagreements, he wasn't sure she wanted anything from him.

She shook her head. How could she talk about how very much she missed Edward? David hadn't shown any anguish over his father's death. If he was grieving at all, she couldn't tell. Whatever he was feeling, whatever was going on inside him, he didn't want to share it with her.

"Tanya, what is it?" he pressed, searching her eyes, wishing she'd talk to him.

"It's nothing." Desperately, she brushed at the tears, trying her best to wipe them away.

He frowned, then used his thumb to brush away another tear. "It's not nothing."

His tender touch caused her to still. Her heart ached for him to hold her, but instead, she pulled away. "It was, uh, it was just the scent of your father's pipe tobacco as I came into the room. It just threw me." Taking a deep breath, she felt a little more in control.

He hadn't even noticed the smell of tobacco in the room, much less connected it with his father. Yet, it had brought Tanya to tears. "You're shaking all over."

"I'm okay, now. Really."

"Really?" The color had drained from her face, and she looked as though she was about to faint. Dark circles were prominent beneath her eyes. His father's death had hit her hard. "Why don't we leave going over the accounts until tomorrow?" he suggested. "You look like you could use a break."

"I'm okay," she said again, but knew that she wasn't. If she didn't get away soon, she was going to start blubbering and make a spectacle of herself. "I know this is something that shouldn't be put off."

"It can wait."

Tanya hesitated. The past few days had been stressful, and she hadn't been sleeping well. The dreams she'd been having were becoming more and more intense. There was the face of someone, a girl, she thought, but she couldn't be sure. When she got up each morning, she felt exhausted, as if she'd just gone to bed. Added to that, she had the pressure of handling her grief and dealing with David. It was becoming too much.

But she didn't dare show any weakness around David. He already didn't think she could manage the plantation. "All right. How about if I bring up the files on the computer and leave you to look them over?" she suggested, thinking that would give her a chance to escape to her room and gather herself together.

"If you want," David answered, watching her.

She gave him a polite smile, then went around the desk. After punching a few buttons on the computer, the screen displayed the file she was searching for. "This file has everything that relates to the plantation. If you have any questions, we can go over them whenever you want." Crossing to the door, she turned and looked back at him. "I'll be in my room if you need anything."

Without waiting for his answer, Tanya escaped through the door to the security of her room. Once inside, she threw herself on her bed and allowed the tears to come.

Three

David entered the dining room and took his seat at the large oak table, surprised that Tanya hadn't yet arrived for dinner. One thing he'd learned about her since he'd returned was she was punctual to a fault. He grimaced. No doubt his father had been responsible for that. His mother had insisted that he and his father be on time for dinner, and after her death, his father had strictly adhered to that rule.

Had that been one of the ways his father kept his mother's memory alive? Shaking his head, David figured he was foolish for attempting to analyze his father. Try as he might, he couldn't equate the unfeeling man who'd raised him with the sad, dying man who had pleaded with him to take care of Tanya. Besides, from what he'd seen, Tanya could pretty much take care of herself.

After examining the accounts of the plantation, David had discovered that she was methodical and efficient and unequivocally honest. Every single expenditure had been meticulously noted and justified. He sighed and sat back in his chair. Her idea to change the farm over to soybeans had been clever. And well-timed. The initial investment had been high, but the money earned after the first two years had covered the cost, plus had returned a nice profit—earnings which had continued to increase.

So he'd been wrong about Tanya.

Again.

First he'd suspected her of having an affair with his father. As if that hadn't been bad enough, he'd practically accused her of trying to steal his father's money. If it was possible to kick himself, he would have. The allegation had been just plain stupid. And to be truthful, he hadn't really believed she'd been sleeping with Edward. He'd been resentful, frustrated over her bond with his own father, a man he barely knew.

And jealous as hell.

But he still wondered if she wanted Cottonwood. Now, to be sure he kept his legacy, he was trapped here for months.

And whose fault was that?

His father's, he silently protested. The man had been obstinate to a fault.

If you'd tried harder to get along with him, you wouldn't be fighting for Cottonwood now. It would be yours. Without strings.

David shook his head. It would have been easier to let Cottonwood go. But he couldn't. There were memories of his mother here, memories of the only happy time in his life.

At the soft creak of the door, he looked up. Expecting to see Tanya enter, he braced himself for the pull of awareness that was becoming so familiar when she was near. When Ruth, his father's cook over the many years, entered, he took a much-needed breath.

Her lean frame contradicted the many pastries, breads and other tantalizing foods she baked. Though the bun behind her head was nearly gray, and despite a wrinkle or two around her narrow lips and soft gray eyes, she'd changed very little. A hint of a smile touched her lips when his gaze met hers.

"Ah, David, I thought I heard you come in." As she neared the table, she placed a generous meal of baked chicken, red potatoes and steamed mixed vegetables in front of him.

David lifted his brow in question. "Tanya's not having dinner?"

The older woman shook her head. "She called from her room to say that she wouldn't be down to eat."

He frowned. When she'd left him earlier, she'd been shaking and upset. He hadn't seen her since. "Is she all right?"

"Is there a reason she shouldn't be?" Ruth countered.

David blinked. "Not that I know of." He changed the subject, determined to put Tanya out of his mind—if only through dinner. "This smells delicious," he commented, breathing in the aroma of parsley, butter and a hint of garlic.

"I hope you enjoy it. I remember how much you used to like these potatoes." She paused and leaned against the large oak buffet.

He grinned. "I still do."

Ruth responded with a reproving look. "Maybe you

should have come home once in a while. I would have cooked anything you wanted."

Caught off-guard by her words, David felt appropriately chastised. His face flushed as he met her gaze. She was right, of course. He could have returned once in a while, made an effort to get along with his father. But it had been easier to stay away and not subject himself to further confrontations and disappointment.

And he'd needed to stay away from Tanya.

If you'd come home, you might never have been able to walk away from her.

And he knew he couldn't have stayed. He swallowed past the knot in his chest. "I know. But my father never cared if I came home or not. The times I called, our conversations always ended in arguments." His father had been one reason he'd stayed away. His attraction to Tanya had been another. But he wasn't going to admit as much to Ruth.

Grunting, the cook glared at him. "That's because you're every bit as stubborn as Edward was. Neither of you was willing to give an inch." With a hand on her hip, she stared him straight in the eyes. "So, you gonna stay this time?"

He shrugged one shoulder. "I have no choice."

"And Tanya?" she asked, concern etched in her expression.

"She'll continue to run the plantation."

Ruth's features relaxed. "Good." She started from the room, then stopped near the door. Turning back, she leveled her gaze on him. "You know, everyone here is very fond of Tanya. She came here as a frightened young girl, and I can only imagine how terrible it must be for her not to remember a thing about her past. Despite the accident that caused her loss of memory, it wasn't long before she was running this place right along with Edward. She earned her position right along with your father's respect."

Her voice was filled with admiration when she continued, "But this last year was especially hard on her. Besides handling the operation of the farm, after your father's cancer was diagnosed, she took him to every doctor's appointment. As his condition worsened, she didn't miss a night sitting with him in his room, catering to his every need. He adored her."

David lifted the pitcher of iced tea on the table and filled his glass, his relaxed manner giving no clue of his clinching stomach. "I know."

Ruth's eyes narrowed slightly. "Do you, David?" She looked as if she wasn't sure whether to believe him. "Tanya is special. I can't say how I know that, I just do. Your father told me he saw something in her, too. That's why he took her in. He saw her potential, wanted to foster it."

"From what I can tell, he did a great job," he stated, his stomach tightening another notch. His father had seen Tanya's potential, but not his own son's. David tamped down on the disappointment that churned through him. Despite his feelings of bitterness for his father, he owed Tanya an apology.

"None of us would like to see that young woman hurt anymore," Ruth said. "God knows she's been through enough."

"I don't want to hurt her."

She gave him a pointed look. "Maybe not, but I remember the way she idolized you."

"That was a long time ago. She was just a kid."

Ruth was quiet a moment, then her eyes softened. "Time doesn't change everything."

As the older woman left the room, David began eating. Her last comment played over and over in his mind. She was wrong, he told himself. She had to be wrong. Because if she wasn't, not getting involved with Tanya was going to be harder than he thought. Almost impossible. Hell, every time they were together he wanted to touch her.

He shoved his empty plate away and drained his glass. What was the real reason Tanya hadn't come down to eat? If she hadn't been hungry, she was probably okay. But what if she wasn't? What if she was ill?

Deciding to check on her, he got up and headed for the stairs that led to the bedrooms on the third story of the house.

The staff quarters were at the back of the house on the bottom floor. The second story had been set aside for guests, and the top floor housed family members. At the top of the stairs, he walked down the hall opposite the direction of his own room and stopped in front of Tanya's bedroom.

"Tanya?" Tapping lightly, he waited for her to answer. When she didn't, he reached for the doorknob, then hesitated.

Should he go in? Maybe not. It was possible that she was sleeping, wasn't it? If so, and he knocked again, he'd awaken her.

But what if she was sick? He thought of all those months she spent taking care of his father. If she wasn't feeling well and needed help, she deserved to have someone looking after her.

He wanted to be that someone, but he knew the

smartest thing to do would be to walk away. Still, the
thought of her being alone and ill made him rap his
knuckles against the door.

Startled by the knock on her bedroom door, Tanya's
breath caught in her lungs. She'd left instructions not to
be disturbed. Who was it?

David?

Oh, God, she couldn't bear for him to see her like
this. If the man knew she wasn't strong enough to handle her grief, he might think she wasn't capable of running the plantation. Then they'd have *that* argument all
over again.

Trying to remain quiet, she buried her face in her pillow to smother the sound of her sobs. Why couldn't she
stop weeping? She'd been in her room for hours, her
sorrow so overwhelming that she'd cried herself to
sleep. When she awoke a little earlier, tears had flooded
her eyes yet again. Her heart ached so badly that she felt
as if she were coming apart inside. She was so tired of
being strong.

When the handle jiggled and the door slowly opened,
she knew David was in her room. Hoping he'd leave, she
held her breath and tried to remain stone-still. She heard
the door close, then his footsteps coming nearer. Her
heart began to hammer in her chest. Despite her desire
to remain quiet, her sob broke the silence in the room.

"Tanya?" David called as he moved closer. Entering
Tanya's bedroom had been an invasion of her privacy,
but he hadn't been able to stop himself. He wanted to
be sure she was okay. Then he would leave.

Turning, he spotted her on the bed. Lying on her side,
facing away from him, she was curled into a tight ball,

sobbing into her pillow. Stunned, he stared at her, only now beginning to realize the magnitude of her grief.

His stomach knotted as he approached her. Not sure of what to say to ease her sorrow, he sat on the edge of the bed, then gently laid a hand on her shoulder.

"Go away!" Mortified, Tanya shrank from his touch. Even as she did, she was aware of how much she wished he'd put his arms around her. Oh, God, she needed so much to be held, to be comforted and assured that this horrible pain would go away.

"C'mon, Tanya," David coaxed, understanding why he'd be the last person she'd open up to. He silently cursed himself. After what he'd accused her of, she had a right to be upset with him. She probably hated him. And rightly so. That he'd caused her worry while she was feeling such heartache shamed him.

Tanya didn't move. "What are you doing here?" she asked, her voice muffled.

"I knocked, but I guess you didn't hear me."

"Yes, I did."

David smiled at the petulance in her voice. She didn't want him there. Well, that was tough. Obviously, she was hurting and needed someone. Though he hadn't been around for his father, maybe he could make up for the way he'd been treating her by being there for her. He owed her that, and more.

He sat on the edge of the bed, both disturbed and surprised that he *wanted* to be there for her. When he touched her shoulder again, she stiffened, but he didn't remove his hand. "Look, I just want you to talk to me."

Tanya sighed as the warmth of his hand seeped into her. Frowning, she thought about how horrible she must look. She sniffed again, then grabbed a few tissues from the box beside her bed and blew her nose. "I'm fine," she lied, tears in her throat. She couldn't bare her soul to David. He hadn't had a loving relationship with his father like she'd had. He'd never understand what she was going through. She fought the urge to tell him how much she ached inside, how much she missed Edward.

How much she wanted, *needed* someone to lean on.

"Obviously, you aren't."

Rolling toward him, Tanya looked everywhere but at his face. "You can't help me," she whispered, wishing he'd leave and wanting him to stay at the same time.

David studied her disheveled appearance and felt something inside him shift. Despite her tousled hair, her puffy eyes and tear-streaked face, she was beautiful. Realizing he was playing with fire, he gently caressed her shoulder, then felt a fist squeeze his heart when another tear fell. "C'mon, Tanya. Maybe I can." Though he'd never been good at relationships, he felt an overwhelming need to comfort her. "I know you're hurting. I'll admit that I don't feel the same depth of emotion for my father, but despite what you think, I'm not made of stone."

She glanced at him, then sighed deeply. Somehow, she found the energy to get up and sit beside him. Her expression softened when their gazes met, and she saw shadows of deep anguish in his eyes. "I don't think that."

She had wondered. He hadn't even talked about losing his father. Why? Maybe sharing her feelings for Edward could help David heal his own pain.

"I miss him," she whispered, and just being able to say those three words made everything she'd been through since Edward's death come rushing back. She closed her eyes against the pain.

"I know you do." He suddenly felt helpless and wished there was something he could do or say to ease her anguish. Though he wanted to pull her into his arms, he resisted the urge, sure she would reject his offer of comfort. His father had never shown him love, nor had he accepted so much as a hug from him.

"It's especially hard now, when we're in between seasons." She looked away. "With winter coming, there isn't as much to do around here, and I can't seem to keep my mind occupied with other things." With so much time to think, everything around her, everything she did, reminded her of Edward.

"And I haven't been very much help," David admitted, stating what she hadn't.

Tanya bit her lip, not wanting to add to his burden. "I know this hasn't been easy on you, either."

She amazed him. She truly did. Even through her grief, she was thinking of him. He wasn't sure what to think. Or do. No wonder his father had cared so deeply for her. David had promised him that he'd look after Tanya. So far, he'd been distrustful, wallowing in his own misery, and he hadn't done a very good job of keeping his word. But if nothing else, he would keep that promise. "Losing someone you care about is never easy. You spent a lot of time with my father."

Tears glistened in her eyes, but Tanya forced them back. "I loved working with him. I know it was hard for you when you came home and found me here, but your father gave me a second chance. I never forgot that, and I worked really hard trying to please him.

"I know you didn't always get along," she continued, realizing the impact of her words would cause him pain. "I heard you arguing with each other when you came home the summer I arrived here. And in the beginning, your father even kept me at a distance. But I didn't have anything or anyone else to focus my attention on, so I pushed him hard, wanting him to show me a sign, any sign, that he liked me." She chuckled through her tears. "He resisted my attempts for a long time, but I continued to chip away at his barriers."

"You accomplished something that I hadn't been able to do all of my life," David stated, surprising himself with the admission.

Touching his arm, she said softly, "I'm so sorry." Tanya hadn't been there when David's mother had died. From comments Edward had made, she knew it had been a painful time. It hadn't been right that he'd shut his son out, but that was the one thing that Edward refused to talk about. Trying to talk to him about how he treated David was when she most often encountered Edward's stubbornness. "You'll probably think this is weird, but I sometimes felt that I filled a void in your father's life, that in some way, I became a feminine influence that had been missing."

"I don't think that's weird at all." Actually, when David thought about it, it made a lot of sense. Maybe his father had responded to Tanya on a level that he could never have reached him on.

"At first, because I was female, he restricted me to working in the house. But I wanted to be with him so I bugged him until he let me tag along. After a while, he began giving me more and more tasks around the plantation. Eventually, he let me work alongside him." She looked at David, her smile a little sad. "At night, after dinner, we'd watch television together." Her eyes brightened ever so slightly.

His lips tipped up at the edges. "He did like his television."

"And he loved working crossword puzzles. There are books of puzzles all over the house. Edward worked one every night. I'd...I'd help—" She stopped speaking, her lips quivering as a fresh batch of tears overwhelmed her. Her shoulders began shaking, and she covered her face with her hands.

"Come here, Tanya." David said, and drew her to him. "Shh, it's gonna be okay."

But she continued to cry.

He held her tighter, and she gave in to her grief. When he stroked her hair, she burrowed closer, pressing her face against his chest as her tears ran unchecked. David held her until she finally quieted and became still in his arms.

"I'm sorry," Tanya whispered, her voice barely audible as she garnered the courage to look at him. She couldn't believe she'd let herself break down like that. And in David's arms. She blinked the last of her tears away.

It felt so good to be held by him, to feel his heat and strength surround her. The solid beat of his heart. Night had fallen, cloaking them in shadows from the moonlight outside her window. She was where she'd wanted to be since she was seventeen.

In his arms.

The intimacy of being in her room, on her bed, made her heart stir with a deep-seated awareness that, until now, she'd kept buried inside. Caught by the need aching inside her, she could no longer control her emotions. She lifted her head, and their mouths were so close, so very close. His warm breath mingled with her own. Her gaze met his. Mesmerized, Tanya stilled, unable to move.

"Tanya," he whispered.

There was a question in his soft tone, but she also heard his desire, saw it in his eyes. His gaze searched hers. Tanya couldn't speak. She simply waited until his mouth touched hers…then she sank into his kiss.

Hot flames shot through her as his tongue slipped into her mouth to stroke and taste and devour. Her breasts tightened as passion overwhelmed her sense of reasoning. She moved closer, wanting more, needing more. Their bodies touched, and Tanya forgot what had brought him to her, why she'd been hurting. His hands slid up her back to her neck, holding her head still as his tongue delved deeper into her mouth.

The sheer pleasure of his kiss consumed every fiber of her being. She wrapped her arms around him, pressing closer, needing him so much that nothing else in the world mattered.

David responded with a groan. He lowered her to the mattress, his mouth pressing hot kisses to her face, her mouth, her throat. When his hand slid up her ribs, she trembled. His fingers found her nipple through her bra, and she nearly came apart.

Arching her back, she gave him access to the clasp, and suddenly it was no longer a barrier. He slid her shirt up, baring her to him. His mouth took her breast, and she went up in flames, the pleasure so intense that she cried out.

Tanya froze, the sound of her own voice reverberating through the room. David was on top of her, his mouth on her breast, his tongue doing wonderful things to her nipple.

She needed to deal with her grief, yes, but not by making love with Edward's son—a man who hadn't shown her an iota of respect since he'd come home. This was wrong. So wrong. How could she do this? How could she be taking pleasure in David's arms when she should have been grieving for Edward?

David raised his head and looked at her. Her face flushed with heat.

"David, let me up," she pleaded, her tone desperate. Oh, God, she'd made a fool of herself. Barely able to breathe, she placed her hands against his chest and tried to push him away.

Confused, David stared at her. His gaze found hers, his eyes dark and glowering. He had every reason to be angry, she thought. But she couldn't deal with his emotions now. She had enough on her hands dealing with her own.

"Tanya—"

"Now. Please!"

Without another word, David rolled off her and stood. He reached out to help her up, but Tanya scooted off the bed under her own power. She couldn't bring herself to look at him.

What must he think of her?

Swallowing hard, she bit back a sob. "Please go." Barely able to get the words out, she turned away from him.

"Tanya—"

"Please. Just leave me alone." Squeezing her eyes shut, she wrapped her arms around herself and lowered her head.

David didn't say anything more. A moment later, she heard her door open, then close. Silence engulfed her, leaving her feeling even more alone than she'd been before David had come to her. It wasn't until then that she realized she'd been holding her breath.

Oh, God, what had she almost done?

Four

Alone, Tanya changed into her nightgown, then practically fell into bed. Despite the exhaustion that made lifting her hand feel as if there was a fifty-pound weight attached to it, she didn't feel at all drowsy. Quite the opposite. Her mind raced with what had just transpired.

For the second time in her life, she'd thrown herself at David. If it wouldn't require so much effort, she'd smack herself in the head. How could she ever explain her actions to him?

You were distraught. It felt good to be held, and he had just been offering you comfort.

Yes, but what had begun as a consoling gesture had spiraled into something much more intimate. Had she been in her right mind, she would never have let him kiss her.

And she definitely wouldn't have kissed him back.

You're lying. You wanted to kiss him.

Her heart stirred as her mind whispered the truth. She really had. She'd wanted so much more than a kiss.

She'd wanted to make love with him. She still did. A heavy sigh escaped her lips. And if she made love with David, what then? He had a life in Atlanta. He'd made it clear that he was only here because he was adhering to the terms of Edward's will. After the year was up, he would leave Cottonwood.

Leave her.

Could she handle his leaving again? Especially now, knowing that her heart was at risk? Getting involved with David would be a grave mistake. Emotional suicide.

He'd hurt her once. Well, yes, she'd been seventeen, young and naïve. But it had still hurt when he'd kissed her as if he truly wanted her, then turned and walked away without an excuse or an apology, dropping out of her life for five long years.

Five years that she'd spent hoping with all her heart that he would return. And she'd let that silly schoolgirl crush ruin her chances of establishing any kind of relationship with a man. God, she hadn't dated another man more than once or twice, couldn't even remember the last time.

At some point, she'd begun passing up opportunities to see other men. She'd refused an offer to go out with Jack Dawson, a banker from the nearby town of Cotton Creek, only last month. She just hadn't been interested. Her life had been busy enough trying to take care of the plantation and Edward. She hadn't had the time or the inclination for anything else.

But the real reason was that Jack wasn't David.

She curled her hands into fists. Why couldn't she stop

thinking about him? Wanting to be with him? The man was infuriating. Not to mention that he didn't even trust her. From the moment he'd arrived, he'd been obnoxious and insulting. Accusing her of an array of wrongdoings. Then, with the cold thoroughness of a businessman, he had busied himself thinking of ways to get rid of her!

Turning on her side, Tanya stared out the window at the moonlit shadows of the magnolia tree outside her bedroom. Face it, she told herself, you're already half in love with him. You've harbored feelings for him for five long years on a single kiss. Lived with the dream that David would come home and make peace with his father, then confess he held feelings for you.

After the way David had kissed her, she suspected that he *was* attracted to her. She sighed heavily. He probably wasn't any happier about that than she was.

So, what should she do? Continue pulling away? Deny herself an intimate relationship with him?

Rolling over to lie on her back, Tanya gazed absently at the ceiling. Okay, damage control. Though not sure of what to do about her feelings for David, she knew that more than likely she would see him in the morning.

First things, first. She'd face David and apologize for her behavior. That would be simple enough to do, right?

She could get through seeing him at breakfast in the morning. She'd tell him that it had been a mistake, that she'd been distraught. Then all she had to do was get through the rest of the day. The next day she'd be leaving to attend a meeting in Washington, D.C. Though she dreaded it, she'd planned the trip months ago, promising Edward that she'd go. It had been hard to do, because she rarely left Cottonwood.

Now she was relieved that she was going. She needed to put some space between her and David, give herself some time to think about her feelings. By the time she returned, what had happened between them would be over and forgotten.

Forgotten?

Really?

Agitated, Tanya turned and slammed her fist into her pillow. Would she ever be able to forget how it felt to have David's arms around her? How it felt to kiss him? To have him touch her so intimately?

Closing her eyes, she tried to block the image of his hand on her body, his mouth on her breast. Instead, she felt an ache deep inside her, a desire so strong that she moaned softly and buried her face in her pillow.

A scream pierced the silence of her room and Tanya bolted upright. Her heart pounded as her gaze swept her surroundings. She was alone in her bed, in her room.

The scream had come from her.

Struggling to breathe, she covered her face with her hands. Drenched in sweat, her nightgown stuck to her, chilling her skin.

Another dream! But in a flash, the images were gone. Just like that. She put her hands against her temples and rocked back and forth in her bed.

Oh, God, what was happening to her? Why was she having these tormenting dreams? And why were they coming more often? The first one had come several months ago and, despite the disturbing feeling it had left her with, she had attributed it to the stress she'd been under. But shortly after, she'd had another, more intense than the first. Now they were coming every few days, each one leaving her feeling more shaken and confused. What did they mean? And why couldn't she remember anything about them when she woke up?

Then suddenly, as if she'd willed it, the face from her dream flashed with blinding speed through her mind. Her body tensed as the image came into focus, then disappeared. A girl! A teenager, she thought, with Kool-Aid-red hair and a silver ring through her eyebrow.

Who was she? It was the same face that had been in every dream. How Tanya knew that, she wasn't sure. Closing her eyes, she tried to focus on what she could remember of the image of the girl. Had she known her years ago, before she'd lost her memory? Was she a sister? A friend?

Tanya tried to concentrate on the dream, struggled to remember more of it, but despite her attempts, she couldn't. Opening her eyes, she took a deep breath and climbed out of bed. Her legs trembled, whether because of the dream or because she'd be seeing David shortly, she didn't know. But since facing him this morning would require her full concentration, she tried to force the dream to the back of her mind.

Running her hands through her hair, Tanya made her way to the bathroom. Catching a glimpse of herself in the mirror, she gasped. Her eyes were swollen and red, her hair a wild mess. Groaning, she twisted the knob for the water, adjusted the temperature to something just short of hot, then stepped into the shower. The steamy spray chased the chill of the November morning from her skin, but did nothing to erase the vivid face of the young girl in her dream from her mind.

After a long shower, Tanya blew her hair dry, then, because it was Sunday and she wouldn't be working outside of the house, decided to leave it down for the day. By the time she'd added a touch of blush to her cheeks and dressed, she felt a little more decent.

Presentable enough to face even David, she mentally convinced herself. Glancing at her watch, she frowned. More time had passed than she'd realized. She hurried to the stairs, noticing that his door down the hall was closed. Great! She had time to get to the dining room first. She wanted the advantage of being seated when he came in.

To her dismay, as she entered the dining room, David was already seated at the table, a newspaper in his hand. She'd assumed his closed door meant he was still inside his room. She wouldn't make the same mistake again.

Starting forward, she felt his gaze on her and damned the misstep in her stride as she walked around the table. In an effort to appear unaffected by his presence, and because she would have looked ridiculous if she hadn't, she took the seat nearest him.

"Good morning." She glanced at him as she scooted her chair closer to the table. His male scent drifted to her. Freshly shaven, his hair was combed neatly, the ends of it still a little damp, making her wonder if he'd just recently showered as well. Like a traitor to her emotions, a vision of what he would look like standing naked in the shower stole into her thoughts.

She swallowed hard. With a great deal of effort, she banished the vision to the back of her mind and gave him a sidelong look. His shirt was an expensive brand, a soft gray pullover, and he'd left the three buttons at the base of his neck unbuttoned, exposing a little patch of his chest hair. Though tempted to continue her appraisal, she averted her gaze.

"Morning, Tanya," David answered, folding the paper in half and laying it aside. He looked at Tanya and his heartbeat quickened. He'd never had a woman affect him just by the sight of her. Not even Melanie. For years he'd suppressed his attraction to Tanya, choosing to live in Atlanta, thinking that if she wasn't available to him, he'd forget her.

But the memory of her kiss had taunted him. The instant he'd seen her, he'd known that he'd only succeeded in temporarily burying his attraction to her. And over the past several days, he was finding it harder and harder to resist the urge to touch her.

After last night, after tasting her again, he was fooling himself if he really thought he could keep his distance. This morning, dressed casually in jeans and a teal sweater, she looked amazing. She'd left her hair free, and the blond strands curtained her face, shielding her expression from his view. All morning, he'd been waiting for this moment, waiting for her. Rising before dawn, he'd hoped to see her at breakfast, determined to catch her in case she snuck out to avoid him.

There was a lot of unfinished business between them. He'd treated her badly since he'd arrived. She should hate him for what he'd said to her the day his father died. Maybe she did. Maybe that's why she'd called a halt to their lovemaking last night.

David couldn't blame her. He ran his hand over the edge of the paper as he looked over at Tanya. She had no way of knowing that he'd figured out that most of his problems and attitudes since returning to Cottonwood had to do with his feelings for his father. Cottonwood was his. He wanted it. He'd never really wanted to leave, but had wanted to salvage some kind of relationship with his father. He couldn't have done that if he'd stayed. Now his life was in Atlanta, not here. And because he'd been so angry at his father, he'd taken his frustration out on Tanya. She hadn't deserved that.

After kissing her last night, nearly making love to her, his attraction was becoming harder to control. He hadn't gotten an ounce of sleep just thinking about all the places he wanted to touch her. What was it about her that was driving him crazy? He could still taste her. But what might happen between them remained to be seen. Right now he had to set things straight between them.

"Look, I—"

"I wanted to—"

Suddenly, they both stopped talking and stared silently at each other. Tanya hesitated, and David seized the opportunity to speak. "If you don't mind," he said, his expression grim, "I'd like to go first."

"All right." Tanya didn't say anything more. She couldn't. Holding her breath, she braced herself. From his dark expression, she could tell he was upset.

"I've been waiting for you all morning." He hesitated a moment, tried to gauge what she was thinking from her look of surprise, then took a deep breath. "I owe you an apology, Tanya. Although there probably aren't enough words to excuse my behavior since I arrived."

Her eyes widened. "What?"

"Despite what you may think, Cottonwood means a lot to me. It's been in my family for years. I thought I was going to lose it. And I was resentful that my father put such a ridiculous stipulation in his will." And resentful that she'd shared such a close relationship with him. When she didn't speak, he went on, "It's just that—" He hesitated, struggling for the right words, then continued, "I was so angry at him. I shouldn't have taken it out on you."

"Oh." Tanya wasn't sure she believed him. Did Cottonwood really mean that much to David? Or did he just not want her to have it?

Despite his apology, she knew one thing was true. David hadn't changed his mind about her being there. Suddenly feeling disconnected, she fought back a fresh wave of tears. Regardless of the kiss they'd shared, regardless of her feelings for him, nothing had really changed between them.

Except now she knew he desired her. She wasn't sure what to think. Maybe she should give up and leave Cottonwood. But if she did, where would she go? She thought of Edward and how much she'd loved him. Because of him, she had a home and a job. David might not like it, but his father had declared it in his will.

David cleared his throat, breaking into her thoughts. She looked up and found him watching her, his gaze intense.

"There's something else that I want to say. I should have said this a long time ago, but—thank you for taking care of my father."

Despite her attempt not to cry, Tanya's eyes watered. "You're welcome." They just looked at each other, caught, it seemed, in a moment. Then Tanya glanced away. Wringing her hands in her lap, she gathered the courage to look at him again. "And while we're on the subject of apologies, I owe you one, as well." She hesitated, biting her lip, her chest aching as the tension inside her built.

David's eyebrows dipped. "I can't imagine why."

"Um, last night, well, what happened...I want you

to know I'm sorry. I was very upset, and I let things between us get carried away."

"Let me see if I understand this. You're apologizing for almost making love with me?" His tone was guarded.

Tanya's gaze flashed to the door with worry, then back to him. "No. Yes. I mean, I know what you must have thought. And could you please keep your voice down? Ruth is liable to walk through that door at any moment."

As if on cue, the door opened and the cook appeared. "I thought I heard voices in here." She placed a platter of eggs and bacon on the table, along with a plate of biscuits. Then she turned to the large oak buffet behind her and retrieved plates and silverware. "Morning, David," she said, giving them each a place setting. "And Tanya, it's good to see you. I trust you're feeling better today?"

After David greeted the cook, Tanya said, "I am. Thank you. And I'm starving. This smells wonderful." She wasn't lying. The aroma of the hot food filled the air, and her stomach growled. She took a biscuit, then passed them to David.

The older woman smiled at the compliment. "Good. Well, eat up. There's plenty. I'll be right back with coffee."

She disappeared, but quickly returned with a steaming carafe of coffee and poured them each a cup. "Ruth," Tanya called as the cook started to leave.

Ruth paused by the door. "Yes?"

"I just wanted to remind you that I won't be here tomorrow."

"Oh, that's right. I believe I have it on my calendar in the kitchen, but thank you for reminding me."

As she left, Tanya busied her hands by buttering a

biscuit. When she finished, she looked up to find David watching her, his expression curious. She chewed, then swallowed. "Oh, I'm sorry, where were we?"

"I believe you were telling me you knew what I was thinking after I kissed you last night," he prompted, knowing that she really had no idea of the depth of what had transpired between them. They'd crossed a line. He'd wanted to make love to her. Not once, but over and over again until he no longer had a breath in him.

Avoiding his gaze, Tanya picked up the platter of eggs and bacon and added a small helping to her plate. "What I mean is, I shouldn't have let you kiss me," she began, flicking a glance at him, then concentrating on what she was doing. "I was feeling so sad about losing your father, and I—"

"You didn't like kissing me," David stated flatly, taking the platter from her and adding a heaping amount of the food to his own plate.

She dropped her fork. Fumbling, she picked it up again. "You're not helping one bit." Frustrated, Tanya glared at him.

He raised his eyebrows. "Sorry. Why don't you talk while I eat?" he suggested, barely able to wait to hear her logic.

"I know you must think I'm terrible. There I was, grieving for your father, and in the next moment, we were practically...well, you know. I don't know what happened. It just felt good to have someone hold me and listen to me."

Suddenly losing his appetite, David stopped eating. "So you're saying that because you were upset, you needed someone to lean on. And I just happened to be there?"

She flushed, relieved that he hadn't alluded to how close they'd come to making love. "Well, yes. I didn't mean to lead you on."

His jaw muscle flinched. So what happened between them meant nothing to her? From the way she'd kissed him, he seriously doubted that. But he didn't challenge her. "I didn't think you did," he replied, an edge to his voice.

"So we agree that it was a mistake?"

David wasn't going to agree to a damn thing. All he knew was that after a taste of her last night, it was going to be harder than ever to keep his hands to himself. "If that's what you want."

Swallowing hard, she glanced at her watch, wanting to make her exit before she did something stupid—like tell him she wanted anything he had to offer. "I'd better be going. I have to make a few calls." She stood, then stopped when her gaze fell to the folded paper beside David. On the cover was a picture of an older man with boyish good looks and dark brown hair. Frowning, Tanya asked, "Who is that? He looks familiar."

Nodding, David picked up the paper, opened it and held it up to give her a better view. "He should. He's Abraham Danforth. He's just been elected to the Senate."

"Oh, yeah, Abraham Danforth." Her head tilted to one side as she looked at the picture and read the headline, *Danforth Heads to the Senate*, above it in large, bold print.

"He won the election. It's been all over the news and in the papers," he replied, surprised she didn't recognize him.

Her brows narrowed into a deep frown. "I knew he won. He's supposed to be at the meeting I'm attending in D.C. tomorrow."

At the mention of her travel plans, David dropped the paper to the table and stood. "Tell me more about this trip. What's this meeting about?"

"The soybean farmers across Georgia have arranged to meet with a committee of congressmen to discuss government controls on exporting and importing and how they're affecting the farming industry. Mr. Danforth..." she stopped, then continued "...Senator Danforth is supposed to be at the meeting, supposedly to lend support to small farmers. I'm looking forward to meeting him." She leaned over the table to get a better look at the picture. "He's quite handsome," she commented thoughtfully.

David's lips twisted. "He's old enough to be your father."

Tanya's gaze shifted to his. "I didn't say I wanted to date him," she stated with an amused frown. "I just think there's something charismatic about his eyes. He intrigues me. I wonder what he's like."

Not liking the way she was staring at the senator, David turned the paper over. "I've never met him, but his whole family has been all over the news lately. Don't you remember that his niece disappeared years ago?" At her look of confusion, he shook his head. "I'm sorry." Through their conversations, he'd seen how hard it was for Tanya to have no memory of anything before her accident. He didn't mean to upset her by bringing up anything that reminded her of her past.

"It's okay. Did they ever find her?"

"Victoria Danforth?" He shook his head. "From what I understand, the family has never gotten over losing her."

Tanya picked up the paper, turned it over and stared at the photograph of Abraham Danforth, unable to take her eyes off it. She couldn't shake the feeling that she'd seen him before.

You're being ridiculous. Of course he looks familiar, she told herself. *He's a public figure.* "That's a shame," she commented.

"Tell me more about the meeting in D.C." She didn't answer, and he realized that she was still staring at the paper. "Tanya?"

"What? Oh." She blinked, then dropped the paper on the table. "Soybean farm owners are invited to speak. I'm hoping to voice my opinions of the current laws regarding importing and exporting. The farmers need the government behind them, not fighting them."

David had learned a lot about Tanya over the past several days. She was smart, determined and loyal, but he couldn't help thinking that she might have trouble holding her own against other, more well-read farmers, and government officials. Had she even been off the plantation for any length of time to learn a skill such as public speaking? Did she even know what she was getting into?

Unable to stand the thought of her being humiliated, he offered, "If you want, I could go in your place."

Already starting for the door, Tanya stopped in her tracks and turned toward him. "What? Why?"

David figured he was more suited to the task, but he wasn't quite sure how to tell her that. "During the course of my work, I've spoken to large groups of professionals many times." He walked toward her, reaching the door and opening it for her.

"And you don't think I'm capable of it?"

So much for being subtle. "That's not what I'm saying."

Her expression cool, she replied, "Well, good, David,

because I think I'm quite up to the challenge. I appreciate your offer, though." Her tone implied otherwise.

"When are you planning to leave?" he asked.

"Early tomorrow morning. Why?" she asked, crossing her arms over her chest.

"Because," he said, his tone resolute, "I'm going with you."

Five

Tanya's heart slammed against her rib cage. "I don't think so."

David's hands went to his hips. He was beginning to wonder why everything they discussed seemed to end in a quarrel. "Why not? You're the one that said I don't know anything about the soybean industry," he pointed out.

"Well, yes, I did, but—"

"What better way is there for me to learn about soybean farming than to go to this meeting with you and hear what the farmers have to say?"

His argument made more sense than she wanted to admit. The problem was, she was already vulnerable to David. After their kiss last night, she knew she'd have a hard time keeping her feelings for him under control if they spent much time in each other's company. She straightened her shoulders, determined to protect her heart. "The best way for you to learn is to be here at the start of the planting season and to follow it through to harvest."

"Thanks to my father, I will be," he retorted, unsmiling. He paused, then after a moment said, "But this is November, and planting season isn't until after the beginning of the year. I'd like to go to this meeting. Consider me your moral support."

Still trying to dissuade him, Tanya continued to resist. "I'll have plenty of moral support. Charlie Pryor, James Dickson and Maggie Bates will be there," she told him, naming a few of the farmers that she knew would be attending.

"Great. I've been away a long time. It'll give me a chance to get to know the other soybean farm owners in the region, hear what they think."

If you go with me, I won't be able to stop thinking about kissing you.

Compressing her lips, she tried to think of another reason, something logical and not insane. "I'm sure you're busy with your business," she finally said.

"I'm capable of multitasking."

"But this meeting has been planned for months." Desperate, she blurted out another argument in an attempt to discourage him. "You probably won't even be able to get a flight."

David was beginning to get the impression that she didn't want him to go. He wondered why. "I'll take the company's plane."

"Your company has its own plane?" she asked, momentarily sidetracked. Apparently she had no idea of the extent of David's wealth. She'd known he was the president of his own company. But his own plane? How big *was* his company, anyway?

Glancing at his watch, David gave her an amused smile. "A jet. With a phone call, I can have it at the Savannah airport in a few hours. You can cancel your flight and go with me."

Flabbergasted, Tanya blinked. "I *can't* do that." She took a step back, placing some distance between them. This was getting way out of hand.

"Sure you can." With one step, he closed the distance she'd put between them. "We can drive to Savannah and fly together. You were going to have to drive to Savannah anyway, right?"

"Yes."

"All right then. It makes sense that we should travel together. Believe me, flying on my plane will be a lot more comfortable than being on a commercial airliner."

Tanya wet her lips. "I've never been on an airplane," she admitted. "At least, I don't think I have." Not since she'd come here to live. And considering that the authorities had described her as a street kid, she doubted she'd ever been near an airport before.

"Never?" he asked incredulously. "My father never took you anywhere?"

She looked away, then met his gaze again. "I've been to a few places, but only by car. Your father often asked me to go on business trips with him, but I never wanted to." Taking this trip would be hard for her, but she had to do it for Edward.

"Why not?" he asked, his expression curious.

"I didn't want anything to happen to me," she admitted quietly. So she'd stayed at Cottonwood, where she felt safe.

David touched her arm, then ran his palm over her shoulder to her neck, stroking her skin until she looked at him. "I'm going, Tanya." His tone made it clear that she didn't have a choice. "And I promise, nothing will happen to you." He'd never dreamed she was afraid to leave the plantation. But considering what she'd been through, he understood it.

Lifting her chin a notch, she met his gaze, not ready to give him his way. "I can do this by myself."

"I don't doubt that, but I'm still going."

She wanted to be angry with him for insinuating himself into her business, but then understood what he *wasn't* saying. The farm was *his* business, not hers. Another reminder, however subtle, that he didn't want her here.

And though she knew it would be better to keep him at a distance, the idea of being with him made her heart skip a beat. His palm felt so good against her skin that she felt her resolve weakening. "It's your decision, of course." As soon as she'd said the words, her heart began to pound.

"Good. Then it's settled." He ran his thumb across her chin, then suggested, "Why don't we go this afternoon, instead? By the time we pack and make the drive to Savannah, the plane can be waiting for us."

Caught off-guard by his suggestion, she stared at him. "I don't know," she hedged, a tingle of pleasure running down her spine where he'd touched her. She could feel herself beginning to give in.

"C'mon. We'll spend the night in D.C. Have a nice

dinner. You'll be more refreshed in the morning if we're already there."

The idea was tempting. Tanya dreaded the thought of getting up while it was still dark to drive to Savannah to catch her plane. And the opportunity to spend time away from Cottonwood with David, away from everything that stood between them, was hard to resist. "All right," she finally agreed.

He touched her hair, wrapping a strand of it around his finger for a moment before letting it go. "I'll make the call."

"Wait!" David had turned away, but he quickly recovered, his gaze meeting hers, his eyebrows raised. "The hotel will be booked. Where will you stay?"

"Where are you staying?" She told him the name of one of the most elite hotels in the heart of the District of Columbia. Nodding, he said, "Most hotels set aside some rooms in case some dignitary or someone famous comes to town. Don't worry. I'll figure something out."

Her heart pounding with anticipation, she watched him walk away.

Hours later, Tanya found out that when David made up his mind to do something, he moved at lightning speed. Sitting beside him as he slowly navigated the streets of the small town of Cotton Creek, on the way to Savannah, she marveled at the holiday decorations already going up on the lampposts and the arches above the streets.

"I love this time of year," she remarked, her eyes bright with excitement. "Especially the Thanksgiving celebration that kicks off the holidays."

David grinned at her enthusiasm and her wide smile. "Don't tell me they still have the annual Thanksgiving Day celebration?" Until he'd left, he'd attended the town's street celebration for as long as he could remember. A vision from his past flashed through his mind, and he saw himself as a child, standing with his mother, waiting with enthusiasm as she bought him a funnel cake. His chest tightened. Funny, he hadn't thought about that in years.

Tanya nodded. "It's this coming Thursday night."

"You're kidding." He could hardly believe it was coming up so soon. Still, his heart stirred at the idea of going with Tanya. "You know, I went every year until I left to go to college."

She turned in her seat to face him. "To meet girls?" she asked with a grin.

His gaze shifted to her, then back to the road. "Cotton Creek isn't all that big. With only one high school at the time, I already knew most of the girls."

"Ah." She couldn't help but wonder how many of those girls he'd known intimately. Enjoying their conversation, she didn't want it to end. For the first time since he'd arrived, they were getting along. "Do you miss Atlanta?"

"It's easier now that I have things set up and I'm able to communicate with my office. Justin West, who's vice president of Taylor Corp. is more than capable of running things in Atlanta without me watching over him. But it's been an adjustment," he admitted. He'd gotten used to a faster-paced life. He stretched his shoulders and noticed that the tension usually there was gone.

There were some advantages to being here, he

thought. And now that he was back, he noticed little things. Like how dark it was at night. And the quiet. No horns honking or cars racing by, no pollution in the air. That hadn't been hard to adjust to.

Tanya bit her lip as she thought over his reply, sure that he still wasn't happy about being forced to live at Cottonwood.

His life was in Atlanta. He was a handsome man, successful and confident, and sometimes, she admitted grudgingly in her mind, he was also quite charming. Certainly there had been someone special in his life during the years he'd lived there. She couldn't help asking, "Have you ever married?"

David looked at her for a long moment, then replied in a flat tone, "No."

Silence fell between them as Tanya digested that information. But she'd noticed the tightening of his jaw when he'd answered. "But there *was* someone special?" she prompted a few moments later.

His cheek flinched again. "I thought so at one time." He thought about ending their conversation right then and there, but despite his reservations, he found himself talking about his broken relationship. "Melanie and I were engaged, but it didn't work out."

"Do you still think about her?"

He gave a harsh sigh. "Not if I can help it."

"What happened?"

He shrugged. "It seemed that she was more impressed by the money I made than by me."

"Really?" Her eyes widened. "What made you think that?"

"Justin. Melanie had been mouthing off to Justin's

date when we went out one evening. Apparently she'd bragged about how easy it was to get what she wanted from me. When Justin heard about it, he brought it up when we were having drinks after work one night. I told him he was crazy. I guess I didn't want to believe it. But I trusted Justin, so I started paying more attention to Melanie's spending habits. I'd given her a credit card with no limit, so it was easy enough to check the bills."

He blew out a breath. "That's when I discovered she'd quit her job months before. Her working wasn't a big deal to me, but I was disappointed she hadn't discussed it with me. I asked her why she'd quit, and she pretty much said because I could buy her anything she wanted and she never intended to work again. I thought again about what Justin had said, wondered how much truth there was to it. So I suggested she get a job and cut back on the spending. She became furious and we argued. Eventually she told me she could find another man to take care of her, one with a lot more than I had to give emotionally."

His stomach muscles tightened. He'd learned a bitter lesson with Melanie that he hadn't forgotten. He wasn't good at relationships. He still believed that was true. After all, he hadn't even been able to repair his relationship with his own father.

Later, he'd rationalized that Melanie's leaving had merely bruised his ego. His gaze shifted to the woman beside him. With Tanya, it would be another ball game. She had the ability to wound his heart. He didn't plan on that happening.

"She must have been crazy," Tanya murmured, then gulped when she realized she'd spoken aloud.

He gave her a surprised look. "I believe you just gave me a compliment." On impulse, he reached over and took her hand. Though he wasn't sure he wanted to know, he asked, "What about you?" He braced himself for her answer.

Tanya's nerve endings came alive at his touch. "I've dated a few men, but no one special."

"Not too many men to choose from around here?"

Because it was true, she nodded. "Cotton Creek has such charm, though. I just can't imagine living anywhere else. I love it here."

As he turned onto I-95, David's gaze narrowed on her profile. He sensed that she'd revealed something about herself without meaning to. She didn't know her past, nothing about her family or where she was from. So out of emotional desperation, she'd made Cotton Creek her home. Tanya had clung to it as if every breath she took depended on it. She'd said as much when she'd admitted that she rarely left. That's why she'd been so angry when he'd suggested that she leave Cottonwood.

It was the only home she knew. He gritted his teeth. He'd almost taken it from her.

He swore beneath his breath. What had he been thinking when he'd suggested sending her away? He'd been so caught up in his own grief and pain that he hadn't thought about how Tanya would be hurt in the end.

Less than an hour later, they took the exit for the airport, and he asked, "Have you been to Savannah before?"

"Only for a brief day trip. You?"

"This is where I came looking for girls." She gave a soft laugh, and when she smiled, if it were possible, she was even more beautiful. "Wanna take a quick look around? I'll give you the cheap tour on the way to the airport."

Her eyes lit up. "Is there time?"

He glanced at his watch. "We've got a few minutes." Taking the next turn, he headed to the Historic District.

They drove past a magnificent house, a mansion of red brick and black wrought iron with a shaded balcony. Tanya stared at the manicured lawn and the bountiful flowers adorning the driveway. "These homes are just beautiful," she murmured as she looked around.

He agreed, pointing out a house on her side of the street with distinct Regency architecture. Seeing how interested she was, he asked, "Would you like to come back for a visit, maybe tour River Street?" He wanted to be the one to show her the city.

Nodding, she said, "I'd love to." They were getting along well, and she was enjoying his company. Too much. For the first time since he'd returned, she felt that their relationship was changing, and despite her reservations about being hurt, she wanted to be with him. A street sign caught her eye, and she turned in her seat to look out, her brows wrinkling as she stared at the tree-lined street.

David drove down a few more streets. He had turned onto Park Street when he heard her gasp. "Are you all right?" His gaze searched hers.

"Yes." Despite her words, she put a hand to her temple.

"What is it?"

"It's silly. I just got this really strange feeling of déjà vu."

"Really?"

"It's nothing," she told him, already regretting mentioning it. "People get those weird sensations all the time. Haven't you ever had one?"

"Yeah." But he'd never reacted to it the way she had, with something close to anxiety.

He laid his arm across the back of the seat as he drove, his hand caressing her shoulder. "You're sure you're okay?"

She nodded and pointed to the clock on the dash. "We'd better go. We don't want to be late." But as she said the words, she twisted in her seat to look at the view outside her window. A sprawling park rolled past them as they drove down Bull Street.

"That's Forsyth Park," he told her when he noticed her interest.

Tanya's brows wrinkled. "Forsyth Park," she repeated quietly.

He nodded. The curious expression on her face made him ask, "Have you heard of it before?"

Her brows wrinkled. "I don't think so." But already she was turning to look at what she could see of the park out the back window.

She didn't know why, but the park had seemed familiar to her in some way. She glanced at David and found him watching her. "I'm okay," she assured him, not mentioning that something about the park had unnerved her. She was having an off day, she thought, because her imagination was really getting carried away.

David turned the car down another street, then another. "One of these streets leads to the airport."

"It's that way." Tanya motioned for him to turn at the next street.

He took the turn, then shifted his gaze to her. "How did you know that?"

"What?" She shrugged. "I don't know. I must have seen a sign back there or something."

He frowned, but kept on driving. Tanya sat back in her seat.

In her heart, she knew she hadn't seen a sign at all.

As promised, David's company jet was waiting for them when they arrived at Savannah's airport. Tanya eyed the small jet with trepidation, but with his assurance that it was safe, she took her seat. When the plane's engines roared to life, her hands tightened on the armrests. She looked at David.

"Don't worry," he told her, then he took her hand in his. "I told you I wouldn't let anything happen to you. Just relax."

Relax? How could she relax with him holding her hand? she wondered. It seemed to her that David was touching her a lot more lately, and truth be known, she was enjoying it way too much. Last night she'd thought that he was going to be angry with her. This morning she'd been shocked when he'd apologized to her. Every time she thought she had him figured out, he surprised her, and she was beginning to like him. Too much.

Instead of worrying about flying, Tanya thought about how good it felt to be with him. The panic of her first flight in a plane was nothing compared to the panic she was feeling about where their relationship might be going. She'd told herself only this morning that he probably regretted their kiss last night. But it seemed that he was finding all kinds of ways to touch her.

"What do you think?" Her look of wonder as the plane lifted off the ground made him glad he'd talked her into going with him. He wanted to see that same look of wonder when he made love to her. For now, he satisfied himself by just gazing at her.

"This is amazing," she breathed. "Just amazing."

"Look," David said, pointing to a mass of water beneath them. Tanya leaned over, straining to see what he was pointing at. Her breast grazed his chest, then settled itself against him. His breath got trapped in his lungs.

"It's beautiful."

"You're beautiful."

Tanya turned her head and looked at him. His eyes darkened to a deep blue, and his gaze locked with hers. At that moment, she couldn't even breathe. As his hand slid behind her neck to the base of her skull, she felt a tingling sensation all over. Her gaze drifted to his mouth, and she licked her lips. She knew he was going to kiss her, and she gave herself to the moment.

His lips touched hers gently, then his mouth settled firmly on hers, teasing, tempting, achingly gentle in exploration. She gave a soft sigh of pleasure when he deepened the kiss, his tongue sweeping into her mouth, dueling with hers, then disappearing, leaving her aching for more.

When his hand slid up her ribs to her breast, the pleasure was so intense, so sweet, that she tried to move more fully against him. Desire coursed through her.

Somewhere deep in her womanhood she felt the embers of a fire beginning. She realized that she was still restricted by her seat belt and the hand rest sandwiched between them. Breaking away, she blinked, then stared at him.

"Damn," David muttered, breaking the tension. "In the future, I'll have to give some thought as to when I make my moves."

Feeling her face flush, Tanya's lips curved into a smile. She settled back in her seat and tried to get her bearings.

Six

Most of the day had passed by the time the plane landed, so they decided to forgo any sightseeing, but David told Tanya that he'd bring her back another time so she could explore the city. Grabbing a taxi, they went straight to their destination, a beautiful hotel in a prominent area. With marble floors and huge white columns, the opulent lobby only hinted at the luxury of the hotel.

David went with her to her room. Tanya drew in a breath as she stepped inside and scanned it. The thick, royal blue carpet was striking against the lemon-yellow walls. Moments after they arrived, there was a knock at the door. David opened the door for the bellman, who delivered her luggage. He handed the man a folded bill, then turned toward her.

"Do you want to have an early dinner?" he asked. She nodded and left it up to him to choose a restaurant. They agreed on a time to meet, and she walked him to the door.

After David left, Tanya opened her suitcase and unpacked her toiletries. She went into the bathroom to freshen up, then slipped on the only dress she'd brought with her, a red silk gown that she'd worn last Christmas. She added a pair of black heels and fastened a diamond necklace around her neck. Lifting the pendant, she fingered it thoughtfully.

Edward had given it to her on her last birthday. Her eyes watered, and she fought back tears. At times the grief still overwhelmed her. But Edward wouldn't want her to be sad. He was, if nothing else, a man who hadn't dwelled on sentiment. Still, it was hard not to cry when she thought about him, and she wondered if David was grieving for his father in his own way. He hadn't even talked about Edward to her. Tanya supposed that wasn't really odd, considering their estranged relationship.

While she waited to meet David, she went over her notes for her talk. Edward would be proud of her, she thought. She'd made it to D.C., and when she spoke tomorrow, she'd be thinking of him and his dreams for Cottonwood.

She heard a knock at her door, so she grabbed her wrap and slipped it around her bare shoulders as she opened it.

"Hi. I'm ready."

His gaze drifted over her. Her red dress hugged her body, exposing every luscious curve. More than anything what he wanted was to back her into her room and strip the damn thing off her. "You look great," he said, instead.

"Where are we going for dinner?" she asked, picking up her purse from the bed.

David told her the name of a popular restaurant not far from the hotel. "Do you want to take a cab or walk?" he asked, hoping she'd choose to walk. If they got into a taxi, he wasn't sure he'd be able to stand being so close to her and not touch her.

"Let's walk," she answered. "It's nice outside, and I'd like to see something besides the inside of the hotel while I'm here."

They left through the main lobby, and David led her a few blocks away to a quaint restaurant sandwiched between a bar and a trendy nightclub. Once they were seated, a waitress took their drink order and disappeared.

"This is nice," Tanya said, nodding at the candle glowing between them. "Have you been here before?"

David nodded. "Once or twice. Are you ready for tomorrow?" he asked.

Tanya sat forward and rested her arms on the table. "I think I am. I looked over my notes. There'll be a lot of speakers, so I'll only have a few minutes."

She didn't seem nervous. Still, he wondered again if she knew what she was getting into. "Is this the first time they've had this kind of meeting?" he asked.

She shook her head. "No, but your father usually went to them. The last couple of years he asked me to go, but I chose to stay home." At the mention of Edward, Tanya noticed David's shoulders tense. She changed the subject. They'd been getting along well, and she didn't want to say or do anything to affect their time together.

As they ate, their conversation drifted from his work to a discussion of the plantation, then eventually again to the meeting they were in D.C. to attend. Tanya looked up over her lasagna and caught David staring at her. "What is it? Do I have sauce on my lip or something?" she asked.

"Your lips are perfect." And they were, he thought, wanting more than ever to taste them again. Struggling to get his mind off making love to her, he grinned and said, "I was just thinking of how different you look from the day I came back home from college and found you living at Cottonwood."

She cringed. "Don't remind me. I wish I knew what possessed me to dye my hair that awful shade of red. It took all summer and several cuttings for it to grow out."

"It was quite punky." He laughed. "Still, I have to admit I was damned attracted to you."

"You were?" Tanya hadn't even suspected. She'd made a point to be around him as much as possible that summer, but he'd acted as if she was a nuisance.

"Judging from your surprise, I guess I didn't send the right message when I kissed you."

She didn't tell him that his kiss had stayed in her memory, that she'd been half in love with him when he left. That it was because of him that she'd never been able to have a relationship with another man. "I thought you hated me. You were so angry that day."

He raised a brow. "Hated you? God, Tanya. I wanted you." More than he'd wanted her to know. Staying at Cottonwood would have cost him his relationship with his father. But their relationship pretty much ended the day he left, anyway.

She covered her face with both hands. After a moment, she'd gathered the courage to look at him. "I've never forgotten the day you left." She flushed when she met his gaze.

"You begged me to stay." His tone was almost somber.

"I was so stupid."

David reached across the table and took her hand in his. "You were a little naive, but not stupid."

Her skin heated at his touch and she sighed. "I wanted you to stay."

"I know," he said, his voice low and controlled. "But I couldn't. My father and I never got along. I thought it would only be worse with him if I stayed."

"Why?" she asked, wanting to know what had caused such a gap between the two men.

He ran his fingers over the palm of her hand. "For one thing, my father and I never saw eye to eye on anything."

"Never?" she asked curiously.

"Pretty much." His lips twisted. "It wasn't always like that, though. I remember when I was young, when my mother was still alive. My father was a different man then."

"How?" she asked, wanting to know more about their relationship, to understand his distant attitude toward Edward.

"The three of us were happy before my mother died. She used to have a fit when my dad would hoist me up on his lap while he worked on the tractor. She was always afraid something would happen to me." He chuckled as he saw a vision of his father and himself. It had been a long time since he'd talked about that, and the memory was bittersweet. "She'd chase after us, and we'd pretend that we were robbers and the cops were after us."

Tanya smiled. "What happened to change all that?" she asked. Surely Edward had had those same memories. What had kept these two men apart?

"My mother died." Sadness stole into his eyes. "When she passed away, my father was devastated. Suddenly, he changed into this person I didn't know. He just shut me out of his life."

Tanya's mouth dropped open. "My God, you were only, what, ten or twelve?"

A muscle worked in his jaw. "Ten. I don't expect you to believe me, but I tried for a long time to get along with him. But nothing I did pleased him. I thought if I left home and was successful at something, he'd at least recognize my potential. I worked hard, started a business and made a lot of money. But all he had to say was that I should have stayed at the plantation, where I belonged."

"I'm so sorry." She shook her head. "I didn't know the man you describe." But now that she thought about it, she'd seen glimpses of him. Whenever she'd tried to talk to him about David, he shut her out and refused to discuss him. "He was stubborn at times, but he'd mellowed so much at the end."

David finished his wine. "I'm thankful that he had you in his life, Tanya."

She blinked back tears at his words. He must have been lonely as a child. For the first time in her life, she was truly angry at Edward. How could he have treated his son so callously?

Maybe she'd been his second chance. Was that the reason Edward had taken her in? Unfortunately, she'd never know. "Do you ever wonder what would have happened if you'd stayed, David? Do you have any regrets?"

David shook his head. "I knew if I stayed, we would end up hating each other," he admitted quietly. "I didn't want to hate him."

Tanya was stunned. She'd been so sure that he hadn't wanted to be around *her*, when salvaging his relationship with his father had been his goal. Her

heart went out to him. "Oh, David," she whispered softly. "I'm so sorry."

He'd revealed a part of himself that she'd never seen
before. For years she'd thought him callous and selfish.
He'd stood there and taken it when she'd accused him
of not caring about his father, not saying a word to de-
fend himself or his actions. She hadn't known that he'd
cared about Edward enough to stay away to preserve
their relationship.

But in the end, David's leaving hadn't made a difference because the two of them had never seen eye to eye.

When they left the restaurant, Tanya shivered from
the chill in the night air. Noticing, David offered her his
suit jacket, and before she could answer, slipped it off
and wrapped it around her shoulders. But instead of letting it go, he used it to draw her to him.

She didn't even think of protesting when his mouth
came down on hers. His kiss was laced with promises,
setting every nerve in her body on edge.

"You taste delicious," he whispered when he lifted
his head.

Tanya couldn't speak. Her heart was hammering as
they walked in silence to the hotel. She found her voice
as they stepped inside the elevator. "I'm glad you talked
me into coming to D.C. early."

He put his arm around her and drew her to him.
"Come up to my suite for a drink." Five years ago, he'd
done what he thought was best and walked away from
her. Tonight, he wasn't going to.

Tanya's heart tripped over itself. It wasn't a com-
mand. But there was no question in her mind what he
wanted. She knew what would happen if she did. But
she couldn't say no, because she wanted him. "All right."

She licked her lips, then looked at him and found him watching her.

David's chest tightened as Tanya's tongue wet her lips, and a burning sensation started low in his belly. He wanted to touch her, but knew if he did, he wouldn't be able to do so without kissing her again. His control when he was around her was slipping, and that scared him. But not enough to let this moment go.

When the elevator reached the top floor, he led her to his room.

"This is beautiful," she commented, her eyes taking in the luxurious sitting area. His room was larger and much more lavish than her own. The view of the city outside his plate glass window was beautiful and romantic. Lights glowed softly for miles.

Coming up behind her, David removed his jacket and her wrap from her shoulders, kissing her neck softly before moving away. "What would you like to drink?" he asked. "There's a minibar, or I can order something from room service."

Tanya shivered and shook her head.

Unable to resist temptation, he pulled her into his arms.

Her lips were soft and inviting, and she kissed him back, her tongue seeking his, kicking his desire for her into high gear. She moved closer to him, pressing her warm body against his. He lifted his mouth from hers, licked her lips with his tongue then nipped at her mouth.

She sighed deeply, and he pulled away, putting some distance between them. "I need to ask you something."

Tanya opened her eyes and met his gaze. "What?"

"This morning you said that it was a mistake when we almost made love last night."

Swallowing hard, she whispered, "I remember."

"I need to know if this is still a mistake."

Tanya didn't answer. Instead, she went into his arms, aligning her body with his, sliding her hand up his chest. She'd waited so long for this day, for this moment, and she wasn't going to let it pass. Though she was playing with fire, at the moment she didn't care. All she could think about was being with him.

David took her mouth, kissing her deeply. Desire exploded inside her. She hadn't been prepared for that. Nor had she been prepared for the heat burning between her legs. She'd wanted this man from the moment she'd seen him, and she wasn't going to deny herself any longer. Whatever happened in the future, she'd deal with it. Right now all she wanted was to make love with him.

He pulled her closer. She breathed in the spicy scent of his cologne. His tongue, hot and demanding, invaded her mouth, dueling with hers, disappearing, then appearing again as if by magic. Never before had a kiss held such promise.

Her body moved against his, and he lifted his head and looked at her. Without speaking, he drew down the tiny straps to her dress, letting them fall off her shoulders. His hands caressed her bare skin as he reached behind her and unzipped her dress. She busied her own hands by unbuttoning his shirt and sliding it off his shoulders.

Seconds later, her dress landed in a pool around her feet. Cool air chilled her skin as she stood practically naked before him. But she wasn't frightened, wasn't hesitant. Her hunger for him exceeded everything.

He drew away, and his gaze slid over her, pausing at her breasts, then his eyes met hers. She felt her face grow hot from his intense scrutiny. "I believe we both have to be undressed to have sex." A small smile played on her lips.

Sex. That shouldn't have bothered David, but it did. However, that thought was quickly lost when he noticed the tightening of her nipples beneath her bra. He felt himself grow hard with need for her.

"We don't have to be, but it's a hell of a lot more fun if we are."

Tanya sucked in a breath as his fingers began unbuckling his belt. He watched her, his gaze almost daring her to look away. She surprised him by reaching behind her back and unclasping her bra. Her breasts jiggled as she freed them from their restraint.

David's mouth went dry. Forgetting that he was still half dressed, he pulled her to him. He didn't want to scare her, but at that moment, he didn't think he could have stopped himself from touching her. He reached out and stroked her nipple with just one finger.

Her eyelids drifted shut, and for a moment he thought she was going to fall. But she opened her eyes again and watched as he took her breasts in his hands, cupping them. He began a slow, erotic massage, and she wobbled a little.

David scooped her into his arms and carried her to the bed. He lay her on it, then shed the remainder of his clothing. When he turned back to her, she raised her arms, the desire in her eyes beckoning him to join her. A small scrap of white lace still covered her. He hooked his fingers beneath the band at her hips and slowly drew her panties down her legs, tossing them away.

Then he went into her arms.

Tanya sighed with pleasure as David's body covered hers. Of their own volition, her hips moved against his.

His hand covered her breast, then lifted it to his mouth. She watched him, and the anticipation of his lips touching her there was almost unbearable.

Instead of taking her breast in his mouth, his tongue licked her nipple, teasing it, tasting it. Tanya thought that she was going to die from the intense pleasure. Need built up in her so quickly that she writhed beneath him. She slid her hands into his hair and pulled his head toward her. He rewarded her by sucking her as he squeezed and molded her other breast. Shockwaves of desire rippled through her body, and she cried out.

David had never felt such urgency for a woman, and he'd never expected such a passionate response from Tanya. He straddled her, then rubbed himself against the most intimate part of her. Her head went back, and she arched against him.

"David," Tanya whispered, feeling as if she was coming apart inside. Her need for him drove her on. She bit her lip, fighting to stay in control, then just as quickly her body began to quiver. "Please," she begged, wanting him inside her.

Leaning over her, David covered her mouth with his own. His tongue dueled with hers as he slid his hand between her legs. He grunted, then hissed out a breath. "Hold on, sweetheart," he rasped. He retrieved the condom he'd put on the nightstand when he'd taken off his pants, sheathed himself, then moved on top of her, positioning himself.

He pushed himself between her legs, testing her readiness for him, wanting her to feel the same intense pleasure that was building inside him. Then he withdrew, building their anticipation. A moment later, he started to enter her again, pushing harder this time. It was then that he realized she was so tight that he couldn't easily penetrate her.

He stared down at her. Her eyes were closed, her face flushed, and her breathing was rapid. Remaining inside her, he cupped her face with his hands. Her hips were pushing against his, and he whispered, "Easy, honey." He pressed a kiss to her mouth. "Tanya, honey, look at me."

When she did, he asked, "Sweetheart, are you a virgin?" It was a struggle to maintain his control.

At his question, Tanya became more coherent and her brows dipped into a frown. Her gaze searched his. "What?" Before he could answer, she understood what he'd said. Her eyes widened with shock. "I don't know," she answered quietly.

Anxiety gripped her. She moved her hips, felt the barrier impeding his entry. The union of their bodies was intensely intimate, but it felt so right that she didn't know even a moment of uneasiness. "I think I am," she whispered.

David began to pull away, but she slid her arms around his waist and held on to him. "Don't. Please don't leave me." She didn't want to beg, didn't want him to know just how much she wanted him, but she couldn't let him go.

"We don't have to do this," David told her. This changed everything. She'd never known a man. He would be her first. The thought of being the first man to touch her stirred his heart. He wanted to be the only man who ever made love to her.

Tanya took a deep breath, then very gently lifted her hips, pushing against his pelvis. "You can't mean that you don't want me. I may not have much experience at this, but I can tell you're aroused."

He chuckled, then kissed her hungrily. Raising his head, he looked right into her eyes. "I do want you, more than you'll ever know. But, sweetheart, I don't want to hurt you."

"Then please don't leave me." Sliding her hands up his arms, she grasped his shoulders. "Make love to me, David."

David sucked in a breath, then covered her mouth in a fiery kiss. He groaned deep in his throat when she began moving against him. Lifting his lips, he whispered, "Let's take it slow." Aching for her, he clamped down on his own desire and began moving his body inside her, slowly stroking her, easing himself into her until he was at the edge of filling her.

She tightened her grip on his shoulders, her fingers digging into his flesh. As if she anticipated his hesitation, she wrapped her legs around his waist, encouraging him. David pushed harder this time, and in one thrust, he entered her completely.

She cried out softly as he filled her, and he stilled, holding himself in check, letting her body adjust to his. He took his time with her, kissing her and stroking her body with his hands until she relaxed.

Then she began moving against him, and he thrust deeper and deeper inside her, molding her buttocks with his hands, holding her against him when she began to lose control.

Tanya closed her eyes and arched up, her hips moving against his. He moved deeper inside her, and the fire that had started building inside her began to blaze out of control.

When she moaned deep in her throat, David could feel her body tightening around his. His own release began spiraling out of control, and he slipped into the black void of ecstasy.

Seven

The room fell silent except for their rapid breathing. Tanya's chest swelled. She knew at that moment that she'd given her heart to him, that he would forever be the man she was meant to love.

She caressed his back, loving the feel of his skin beneath her fingers. He groaned, went up on his elbows and looked at her. When their gazes met, she smiled up at him. "So are those the moves you used to put on the girls?"

He chuckled, then briefly kissed her mouth as he pinned her to the mattress. "I never got results like this. You were amazing."

"You were pretty amazing yourself," she answered.

Sucking in a hard breath, he tried to gather a modicum of control. Making love with Tanya had staggered him. More than ever, he knew his heart was in danger. But despite his inner warnings, he wanted more of her.

"Are you all right?" he asked, tilting his head down to look at her.

Her gaze drifted to his mouth. "I am now." She ran her tongue along her lips, still tasting him, and her body quivered. Closing her eyes, she relished the moment, not allowing herself to feel regret. For five long years, since she was seventeen, she'd dreamed of the day David would take her in his arms and make love to her.

That she wanted him to truly love her was undeniable. She already loved him. Truth be known, she'd loved him for years. Though her heart ached for it, she hadn't expected a confession of his undying love. For the moment, she was content to be with him, and she wasn't going to let anything ruin this moment.

He quirked an eyebrow. "Are you sure?"

She nodded. "I think I might need a quick shower," she told him, then felt heat rise to her face.

David kissed her mouth, then raised himself up over her. He met her eyes. "Stay put." He rolled off her and stood beside the bed. His gaze raked her body and his gut tightened.

He wanted her again.

Now.

But he knew it was too soon for her to make love again.

"I'll be back in a minute." He went into the bathroom to clean up, then reached over and turned on the water in the tub. It took a few minutes for the water to heat, then he adjusted the temperature and pulled the knob for the shower. He returned moments later to the bedroom, and before she could speak, he scooped her into his arms.

"What—"

"Shh," he said, then proceeded to carry her into the

bathroom. Setting her on her feet, he stepped inside the shower, then tugged her in with him.

Tanya started to protest, then swallowed the words when the warm water and steam surrounded her. David maneuvered her until she was beneath the spray. "Mmm, this feels good," she murmured.

A dispenser on the shower wall provided shower gel, shampoo and conditioner. She watched in silence as he pushed the button for the gel, then lathered his hands. Then he began washing her body, beginning at her shoulders, working down her body until he reached her thighs. The feel of his hands moving so intimately on her started a fire smouldering in the center of her womanhood. Her teeth clenched. "I can do this, you know," she told him, wanting him to stop touching her before she made a fool of herself and begged him to do more than just wash her.

He gave her a grim look. "I wanted to be sure you were okay."

"We had sex, David. I'm a little tender, but it didn't make me an invalid."

Sex. There was that word again. He gritted his teeth. "It was your first time." Then he frowned. When she'd been brought to Cottonwood, his father had been told that she was a juvenile offender. If she'd been in trouble and had traveled in bad circles, how had she remained a virgin? It didn't quite fit her image as a street kid.

Tanya wanted to tell him she was all right, but he lathered his hands again and began stroking her between her legs, easing the ache there. It was all she could do to continue standing.

"How are you feeling?"

"Like I want to make love with you again."

"It's too soon," he told her, then kissed her briefly.

"I'm fine," she told him, giving him a small smile. "Did you think I wouldn't be?"

He put his finger under her chin. Lifting her face, he examined her through the steam. "I wanted to be sure." When he was done, he turned her toward the running water and she rinsed herself.

As he began to wash, she got out of the shower and started drying herself. Before she finished, he was turning off the water and stepping from the tub. "Here, let me do that," he told her, taking the towel from her and motioning for her to sit on the toilet so he could dry her hair. When he was done, she took a few minutes to work out the knots and comb it back from her face.

She walked back into the bedroom, a towel wrapped around her body. David had stripped the bed.

"We'll sleep in the other bedroom tonight," he stated, looking at her.

She felt her cheeks grow hot. "Oh." So he'd assumed she wouldn't be going back to her own room. At another time, Tanya might have resisted his taking control and assuming that she would be spending the night with him. But she didn't argue because the idea of sleeping in his arms made her heart pound.

And she was greedy. She didn't expect this time with him to last. When he left her, left Cottonwood, her heart would suffer. She wanted every moment she could have with him.

David awoke with a start, instantly aware something was wrong. He saw Tanya beside him, thrashing about in her sleep. Grabbing her arms, he tried to subdue her.

Her chest heaved and she struggled to breathe. Then she screamed and her eyes flew open.

"It's okay, honey," David crooned, trying to calm her. Obviously she'd had some kind of bad dream. To his surprise, Tanya burst into tears. For a moment he was stunned, and he wondered if she was hurt. A quick assessment of her assured him she wasn't. He pulled her into his arms. "Hush, sweetheart. You're all right. I won't let anything hurt you."

Tanya sniffed, then battled for control. It was a few minutes before she could speak. When she did, her voice trembled. "David, I had the strangest dream. I can't describe it all, but it was so real."

"What the hell was it?" he practically growled, feeling anxious and inadequate at the same time.

She took a deep breath. "I'm not sure. I was at this house, but the weird thing is that I felt as if I'd been there before. There was a celebration, a birthday party, I think."

Trying to calm her down, he said, "It was just a dream, honey. Don't let it upset you."

"No, it was more than that, David," she told him fervently. "It was almost as if I belonged there, like it was a vision or something."

He tightened his embrace. He wanted to be supportive, but was skeptical of anything involving the supernatural. "I'm sure it was nothing." He reached over and turned on the light. "Just take a deep breath," he said. "You'll feel better."

Blinking from the light, she rubbed her eyes, then focused them on him.

"I'm not making this up."

"I didn't say—"

She sat up and put her hand in front of her, palm out. "Just listen." Tanya hadn't told anyone of her other dreams, or of the strange things that had been happening to her lately. But she wanted to tell David. She wanted him to know, wanted him to help reason out what was happening to her. "It wasn't the first one. I've had several strange dreams lately, and each one is becoming more vivid than the last. In this one, I saw myself at this house, but the odd thing is that it didn't feel wrong for me to be there."

David sat up, too, and he took her hand in his. "Tell me everything."

Tanya did, recounting every dream she'd had, especially the one with the strange girl she'd had last night. She told him about the strange sensations she'd been having over simple things. Like the odd feeling that she'd had when she'd seen the picture of Senator Danforth, and knowing which way to turn when they'd been heading to the airport. She finished by admitting that she had the feeling she'd been at Forsyth Park before. "What does all this mean?" she asked. "It's driving me crazy!"

"I don't know," David said, shaking his head, trying to make sense of everything she'd told him. He'd never been one to believe dreams had much significance. Now he wasn't so sure. Tanya was trembling, and he wondered if something, however unusual, was happening to her.

He studied her and an explanation dawned on him. "The amnesia." He said the words softly, so as not to traumatize her. "Maybe, and I mean this is only a possibility, maybe your memory is returning."

Shock at his explanation almost numbed her. "Oh, my God." Her heart began to pound so hard that she put her hand to her chest. "Oh, my God, David. Maybe you're right!" she exclaimed, and her voice rose to a high pitch. "The peculiar dreams, the feeling that I've been someplace in Savannah before. Even here in Washington," she said in a rush, "I've had that same sense of awareness."

David caressed her face. "Don't get too excited," he told her, trying to calm her down. From her exhilarated expression, he saw it was already too late.

Her eyes grew bigger. "No, you're right! That's the only explanation. It is! It must be that!"

"It's a reasonable conclusion to us, but it may not be that simple, Tanya. They could be happening for any number of reasons. I don't want you to get your hopes up because all this could still be just a coincidence." He wrestled with the idea of her memory returning for a few moments, then realized, selfishly, that he wasn't sure that getting her memory back was such a good thing. How would it affect things between them?

She'd had a life before she'd come to Cottonwood. Considering her past juvenile record, maybe it hadn't been such a good one. Maybe she wouldn't want to remember everything. And what if that old life appealed to her? What if she wanted to return to it?

When he'd first come home to Cottonwood, David had wanted to send Tanya away. He would have done anything to make it happen. Because his feelings for her were all tangled up with the plantation and his father. And she had a way of keeping him on guard all the time. But now the idea of her leaving bothered him more than he wanted to admit. Even to himself.

"Let's not jump to conclusions," he told her firmly. "I want you to get a checkup as soon as we return home."

Home. Tanya blinked. The way he'd said it made her wonder if he was beginning to think of the farm as his home. It was too much to ask for. David was right, though. She needed to be examined by a doctor. Suddenly she sobered. The thought scared her a little. What if she didn't like the person she'd been? Worse, what if David didn't? She'd had a checkered past, so she must have lived a wild, maybe even violent life. Would getting her memory back mean losing what she was just beginning with David?

Hours later, Tanya lay in David's arms, her head resting on his chest as he held her. Being with him felt so right that she couldn't muster the strength to leave his side. He'd made love to her again, this time using the skill of his hands and mouth to bring her to climax, whispering that she wasn't ready for anything more strenuous. She'd protested, insisting that she was fine, but he'd been adamant and had shown her other ways to enjoy their intimacy.

Though he'd resisted her attempts at intercourse, what she'd experienced with him had been wonderful and fulfilling. She'd used the same techniques to explore his body that he'd taught her while pleasuring hers, and they'd been exhausted by the time they were finished.

Her body was sore, and though he'd insisted she wasn't ready to be with him again, she'd wanted him inside her. Making love with him had been wonderful, but it had also forced her to face reality. Which made her think even more about where their relationship was going. Besides beginning a physical relationship, nothing between them had truly changed.

She was hopelessly in love with him.

Believing he was still asleep, she stirred, then began to move away. His hand clamped around her hip, pinning her in place. She looked up at him and smiled. "I thought you were asleep," she murmured.

He didn't answer. Instead, he claimed her lips in a long, drugging kiss. "Where are you going?"

"I need to start getting ready," she told him. "The meeting starts in a couple of hours."

"Get ready here," David said, "with me." He didn't want her to leave, didn't want to lose the closeness they'd found.

"I can't." She slid her hand over his chest. Enjoying the freedom of touching his body, she ran her finger through the coarse hair there. "My clothes are in my room."

Together they climbed from the bed, and Tanya was surprised at her lack of inhibition as she stood before him naked. Her gaze slid down his body, and a lump formed in her throat. Her love for him was even stronger now that she knew what it was like to be intimate with him.

"I'll shower first, if you want, then dress while you're in there." She walked around the bed toward him.

He pulled her against him, cupped her breast with his palm. "Let's shower together."

Licking her lips, she looked at him. "I have a suspicion that we won't just bathe," she whispered, then her lids drifted shut when he began kissing her neck. It took all of her willpower to push out of his arms. "I don't want to be late."

He smiled lasciviously. "You're right."

Tanya scooped up the dress she'd worn to dinner, then headed to the bathroom. David watched the sway of her hips as she disappeared inside and shut the door. Though he knew that she didn't want to be late arriving at the meeting, he was damn tempted to interrupt her shower.

About fifteen minutes later, she came out of the bathroom in her dress, her blond hair combed straight. "I'm going to my room to finish getting ready," she said, slipping on her shoes. She glanced around for her bra and panties, but they were nowhere to be seen. Rather than make an issue of searching for them, she figured she'd find them later.

When she started for the door, David stopped her, pulling her against his hard body. His mouth came down on hers, claiming her lips in a possessive kiss that made her toes curl. "I'll see you in a few minutes," she whispered when he lifted his lips.

With reluctance, he let her go. "I'll come to your room to pick you up," he told her, kissing her again, then letting her leave.

An anxiousness filled him as he went into the bathroom. It was something intangible, but it was there just the same. He knew it had to do with Tanya's amnesia, knew that despite his warning for her not to get excited, her memory was returning.

Instead of feeling good for Tanya, he worried about the repercussions. If indeed she was remembering her past, he didn't want Tanya to be disappointed or upset by what she learned.

Though he doubted what was between them could last, he wasn't ready to lose her to her former life.

"Are you ready?" David asked a little later, as they waited for the meeting to begin. He thought that he'd had a good idea of what Tanya would face when she'd said she was planning to speak at the committee meeting on soybean farming. She'd explained to him that there would be a large conference room filled with people interested in soybean farming—some who were experienced farmers, and others just here for information.

David shook his head. Now he had a better understanding. The room, reserved in one of the finest hotels in the heart of the District of Colombia, held hundreds of people. At the front, a row of tables divided the group of dignitaries seated behind it from the mass of people in rows of chairs across from them.

Tanya gave him a confident look. "Yes, I'm ready."

With what he termed a polite smile, she turned her attention to the speaker and looked as if she was straining to hear what he was saying over the murmur in the room from her seat at the back. "Your turn's coming up next."

"I know," she replied, barely glancing at him.

Despite her assurance, he wondered if she knew what she was getting into. She seemed confident, that was obvious. Still, he couldn't help thinking that although she had a good knowledge of soybean farming, he doubted she had the ability to speak in front of such a large and dignified group. He didn't want to see her embarrassed or humiliated. His feelings for her had been constantly changing since he'd returned home, and making love with her had only confused him more. But one thing he couldn't deny. He was beginning to care deeply for her—more than he felt was safe for his heart.

On their way down to the meeting from her room, he'd again offhandedly offered to take her place as the speaker. She'd promptly refused, insisting she could do it. Looking around the room, he couldn't help but have second thoughts. During the drive to Savannah and during dinner last night, they'd talked in depth about the effect government controls had on soybean farming. He wanted to offer to speak on her behalf again, but he didn't want to undermine her confidence.

"Are you nervous?" he asked, wondering if she'd even admit it if she was.

Rolling her eyes, she gave him a sidelong glance. "Shh. No, I'm not nervous. When I'm up there, I'll just imagine you naked," she told him with a teasing smile.

David leaned very close to her ear and whispered, "Then don't look at me, because if you do, I may just come up there and drag you back to our room."

She slid her tongue out of her mouth and slowly traced her lips, her grin wicked. David felt his temperature go up a hundred degrees as she turned her attention toward the front of the room. Trying to concentrate on the speaker at the podium, instead of his hard groin, he listened for a few minutes as the man answered a question from one of the senators. Caught off-guard and unprepared, the man stumbled over his response. Becoming even more concerned about Tanya's turn, David touched her arm. "Are you sure you don't want me to do this?"

She turned toward him and gave him a tolerant look. "Don't worry. I know what I'm doing."

Before he could say anything more, her name was called over the loudspeaker. Tanya stood and made her way to the front of the room. David watched her in awe, her graceful stride holding his gaze. She was easily the most beautiful woman in the room. He couldn't take his eyes off her as she stepped behind the podium and introduced herself.

At the sound of her voice, a hush fell over the crowd. David glanced quickly around him and noticed that all of the participants had turned their complete attention to her. She began to speak, her voice eloquent, her tone firm. David listened to every word and was impressed by her ability to get her point across. Poised and confident, she fielded question after question by the government officials, her answers concise, carefully worded and convincing.

David stared at Tanya, his mind spinning. He'd seen women who had attended finishing school, who had earned graduate degrees, who couldn't speak as well as she could. Where had she learned the skill of public speaking?

Or had she come by it naturally? He couldn't understand it. From what they'd been told of her background, it just didn't make any sense.

She left the podium amidst the loud clapping and cheering of the crowd, her smile appreciative and pleasant as she slid into her seat. Still taken aback by her composure, David took her hand, then threaded his fingers between her slim ones. Her amber eyes met his, shining and excited with energy.

"You were amazing!" The word was, of course, inadequate for what he really wanted to say to her. He was ashamed that he'd thought her incapable of carrying this off. She'd done that and much more. With her knowledge of soybean farming, she'd been more effective than he ever would have been. "You practically had the members of congress eating out of your hand."

She shrugged her shoulders. "I think I got my point across. At least, I hope I did."

"Sweetheart, I watched them. You did a hell of a lot more than that. It was obvious by their expressions that they were really impressed." He hesitated. "Hell, *I'm* impressed," he admitted as they waited for the next speaker to begin.

Her smile was indulgent. "You thought I'd fall on my face?"

"Not exactly, but I'll admit that I was worried. Now I see that it wasn't warranted." He'd been smiling, but his expression sobered. "Tanya, you handled yourself better than many people that went to school to learn to speak in public. Where did you learn to speak like that?"

Pleased by his praise, she blinked. She'd never given any thought as to why she wasn't hesitant to speak. She'd been more worried about leaving Cottonwood. "I don't know. I knew what I wanted to say. I'd like to think I don't intimidate easily."

David knew that was true. He'd given her hell more than once since he'd returned to Cottonwood, and she'd held her own against him every time. Was her ability to speak publicly in a professional setting yet another peek at her former life? It couldn't be, he reasoned, because it certainly didn't correspond with the description of her as a troubled teen.

He was learning that there were many facets to this woman. There was a lot about Tanya that he admired and respected. She was caring and had been fiercely loyal to his father. At every turn, she surprised him with her intelligence and self-assurance. He'd never met a woman he wanted more.

And for the first time, he wondered if he'd be satisfied by an affair.

Eight

"What do you think happened to Senator Danforth?"

Tanya frowned. "I don't know. I was disappointed that he had to cancel his appearance at the meeting," she said as she and David lay in bed talking. She slowly ran her hand over his arm. The meeting had ended a little earlier than planned, so they'd collected her things from her room, then had returned to his room with plans to go to the zoo.

They never made it.

David had pulled her against him and kissed her as if he'd been starving for the taste of her. Tanya had quickly forgotten their plans as they began to undress each other. Eager to be loved by him, she planted kisses on his neck and chest as he shed his shirt, then pressed her lips along his belly as he tugged his slacks down. They'd fallen into bed, and this time David hadn't held back. He'd worshiped her body, then when she was crazy with wanting him, he'd entered her and loved her until she cried out his name.

Now exhausted, they lay in each other's arms, leisurely stroking each other. Tanya had never been so happy.

"I was disappointed I didn't get to meet him. There was something strange about him not being there, but I can't exactly say what makes me feel like that," she told David. "It was almost as if his presence meant something more than just support for soybean farmers."

"I'm sure whatever prevented him from attending was important. Probably something pressing that had to do with his Senate seat," David speculated, noticing that her eyes were actually sparkling. He wondered whether it was from her success earlier in the day or from making love.

Tanya yawned and snuggled closer to him, seeking his warmth. "Probably."

David smiled down at her. If he could summon the energy, he'd satisfy himself with her body again. While at first shy when making love, she'd quickly become accustomed to him touching her, responding eagerly when he'd stroked her and brought her to climax. She'd become eager to learn and take part in their lovemaking. Tanya was surprisingly passionate, and he was having difficulty keeping his feelings for her under control.

He'd thought that once he'd made love with her he'd be able to get her out of his system. However, the exact opposite was happening. She was all he thought about, and he'd even begun imagining what it would be like if he stayed at Cottonwood.

David wasn't sure he could do that. The memories of his father were painful. It was hard not to associate

Cottonwood with years of disappointment and heartache. He'd always wanted to stay and work the plantation with his father. Now that his father was gone and David could stay, he had a successful business in Atlanta, another life away from the farm.

But Tanya belongs at Cottonwood, a voice inside him whispered. When it came time to leave, would he be able to walk away from her?

Tanya sat in silence as their plane began to make its descent to Savannah International Airport late in the afternoon. As she and David had prepared to leave Washington, uncertainties of where their relationship was going pulled at her. While she was in love with him, his feelings for her were less tangible, and she worried about how they might change when they returned home.

Would returning to the plantation, which held so many unpleasant memories of his father, make David withdraw from her? In Washington, they'd been away from everything that reminded them of Edward's will and the stipulation that forced David to move back home. How would he feel about her when he was forced to remember his father's prerequisite to his inheritance? Did he still harbor bad feelings about her being there? Did he still resent her managing the plantation?

He didn't love her. She wasn't going to pretend that he did. But he desired her, and she prayed that he might grow to love her if he gave their relationship a chance.

Turning to look at him, Tanya's heart swelled. She had no idea where their relationship was headed, but she was powerless to protect her heart.

She loved him. So much. Still, she held the words inside, knowing it was a mistake to say them.

David didn't love her.

He cared for her. He wanted her.

But he didn't love her.

She wasn't going to complicate things between them. Wasn't it possible that one day she'd mean more to him? They had more than eleven months to live together. Their relationship had been rapidly changing. A week ago she'd believed he hated her, and now they were lovers.

Hope filled her. She'd enjoy the months ahead of her, enjoy being with him.

And maybe one day he'd fall in love with her.

Tanya felt a sense of accomplishment as they arrived back at Cottonwood. In retrospect, she thought it silly that she'd been apprehensive about leaving the farm. Just because something tragic had happened to her once didn't mean that it would happen again. Still, she was glad to be home.

David got out of the car when she did, and he popped open the trunk and retrieved their luggage. It wasn't until they went up the stairs that she began to feel a little anxious. He stopped at the top of the stairs and put his own luggage down, then followed her to her room and placed her bags in a corner of the room. They hadn't talked about the change in their relationship, and she wondered what he was thinking.

She needn't have worried. He pulled her against him, kissed her hungrily, then told her he was going to put his own things away. Catching her breath, Tanya watched him leave, her heart encouraged.

After unpacking, she went to the office to check the mail. Sharing the space with David had been difficult before they'd left, as she'd tried to do her work when he wasn't there. Now she walked in, saw him at the desk, and smiled. "I thought I'd call the doctor today and see about getting an appointment," she told him as she approached him.

David looked up. "Who's your doctor?"

"I've been to Dr. Brewer, your father's doctor, a few times. I really haven't had much of a reason to go to a doctor while I've been here. Besides the amnesia, I've been pretty healthy."

"Have you been thoroughly examined since you arrived here?"

"They did a lot of tests on me when they found me, but I've had no reason for any further testing."

"Then I'd like to take you to Atlanta."

"Atlanta?" Her brows wrinkled. "Why? Certainly there are doctors in Cotton Creek that I can go to."

"I'm sure there are, but it might be hard to get an appointment right away. I just got off the phone with Justin. Something's come up and I need to make a quick trip to the office for a meeting. You can go with me. I have a friend who's a neurologist. I want you to see him."

Her eyes filled with confusion. "Do I need to see a specialist?"

David stood and came around the desk, then tugged her into his arms. He kissed her and looked into her eyes. "You need to be examined by an expert on brain injuries. Considering what's been happening to you, I want you to see someone right away. You might need to have some tests. We can get all that done in a day or two in Atlanta. It could take weeks here."

His argument made sense. Besides, she was curious about his life in Atlanta. Going there with him would give her an opportunity to see where he lived, maybe see his office and meet some of his friends. Still, she hesitated. She'd been looking forward to spending Thanksgiving here with him. Then there was the town's celebration. She didn't want to miss it. "When would we have to leave?"

David rubbed her back with his hands, bringing her closer to him. "In the morning."

She groaned. "I've just finished unpacking." She gave in when she saw the determination in his eyes. "All right, but you have to promise that we'll be back by Thanksgiving. I want to go to the celebration."

"I promise," he whispered, then moved against her, his intent obvious.

Tanya's eyes grew into big circles. "David!" She glanced at the open door. "Someone could see us," she exclaimed, her cheeks turning red.

"We'll shut the door," he whispered as he began kissing her neck.

Tanya thought that was an excellent idea. Relieved his desire for her hadn't diminished, she went to the door and locked it. Eager for each other, they stripped out of their clothing, then came together in a heated rush, his mouth crashing down on hers, drugging her with his kisses. David maneuvered them to the sofa and eased her onto it on her back. A frenzy of lovemaking ensued as their bodies met and moved together, until David was nudging her legs apart. He entered her with one hard thrust, then pushed deeper and deeper as his hips drove against hers.

Tanya locked her legs around his waist and hung on, straining against him to reach that elusive peak, then suddenly her body quivered with surrender. David's release came only moments later. Afterward, as they lay together, Tanya knew there would never be another man for her.

The Atlanta skyline lay before them as Taylor Corp.'s jet eased down to the runway and landed on the tarmac. Tanya began to feel more and more uncomfortable about being in Atlanta, but if someone had asked, she wouldn't have been able to say why. A sensation of foreboding had settled inside her, and she just couldn't shake it.

David took her hand in his as the wheels of the plane squealed to a stop. She smiled at him, hoping her nervousness didn't show.

A few minutes later, her eyes widened as she stepped out of the plane and went down the steps. A sleek black luxury car was pulled up nearby. The driver, a handsome, well-dressed man, got out and circled the front of the vehicle. He looked to be about David's age, maybe a little older, but he was taller with a lean frame. His dark suit fit his broad shoulders, then narrowed at his trim waistline. A broad smile spread on his lips as they reached him.

"Welcome to Atlanta," he said to Tanya, taking her hand in his.

Tanya knew from the moment he'd spoken that she'd like him. There was no other word for him except *gorgeous*—the kind of man that might have caught her eye if her heart hadn't already been taken by David.

David's glance flitted from Justin to Tanya, and his gut tightened. Having been friends a long time, he knew the number of women who passed through Justin's life. While his friend wasn't flirting with Tanya, he was damned close. Taking her arm possessively, David introduced them. "This is Tanya Winters, Justin. Tanya, Justin West, my friend, and vice president of Taylor Corp."

"It's a pleasure to meet you," Justin said, then gave his friend a long look before shifting his gaze back to Tanya. "David said you were beautiful," he told her, his tone sincere, "but I don't think the word does you justice."

She smiled at him. "Thank you." She gave David a sidelong glance. So he'd talked about her with Justin. She wondered in what context.

Justin turned to David, then gestured toward the car. Once they were seated, David and Justin jumped right into business. "Delgado is one tough customer. You have a meeting set up with him in one hour at the office," Justin informed David.

"This merger will give him a greater customer base with the added luxury of decreased overhead. That alone will generate millions for him."

"We've talked in depth about that, but his feathers have been ruffled. He thinks he's not important because you haven't been here," Justin told him as the car headed toward downtown Atlanta.

Tanya listened as the men talked, and it became apparent to her that although David had been running his business from Cottonwood, it hadn't been easy. Obviously he was used to being in the thick of things. As he talked with Justin, his whole demeanor changed. He shifted into a different mode of performance. Watching the changes in him, she wondered how much he missed the world he'd created for himself.

He was living at the plantation out of necessity, not out of choice. After they'd made love, she'd let herself hope that he could be happy at the farm. But would that really be an option for him? Though he'd seemed interested in the workings of the plantation, his interest probably stemmed from the need to know more about his newly inherited business and not from his personal interest. Discouraged by her thoughts, she stared out the window at the passing scenery. She was fooling herself if she thought that he would one day want to live on the plantation.

The car slowed and parked in an underground garage on Peachtree Street. Tanya followed the men inside a tall, impressive glass-windowed building.

"I also called Lucas," Justin said, then looked at Tanya and explained, "Lucas Avery is a friend of ours. He practices here in the city."

"What did he say?" David asked. He pushed the button for the elevator. A moment later, the doors opened and they stepped inside.

"He made some time for Tanya at two o'clock today. If that's okay with you," he commented to Tanya. "While David is meeting with Delgado, I'll take you to Lucas's office." He paused, then added, "I hope you don't mind that David mentioned your amnesia to me."

Tanya shook her head. "No, that's fine. I appreciate your calling someone for me." She did. She thought it was nice of him to offer to take her. But she would have preferred David accompany her.

The elevator doors opened with a *swish*, and they stepped into an impressive foyer. She walked across the beige marble floor, following the men through a door, then down a hall. David spoke to several people, then stopped in front of the desk of a dark-haired woman who appeared to be in her late twenties. She had a generous mane of black hair and eyes the color of a blue, summer sky. *Striking* was the word that came to mind as David introduced them.

"Jessica, this is Tanya Winters. Could you show her to my personal quarters?" He turned to Tanya and said, "There's a room off of my office where you'll be more comfortable while you wait. I have a few things to go over with Justin before my meeting begins. Jess will take care of you. Let her know if you need anything."

"I'll be fine." She watched the two men walk away, then looked back at Jessica. David had shortened her name to Jess, and Tanya wondered whether his familiarity came from working with her or from a personal relationship.

With what appeared to be a frozen smile, the woman withdrew a key from her desk. "Please come this way," she said, her tone professional as she came around the desk and led Tanya down a hall. Stopping in front of a closed door, she opened it with the key. "After you," she said, then followed Tanya inside the room.

Tanya's gaze swept the small room. It had a large gray sofa that practically took up one whole wall, a coffee table, a recliner and little else.

Jessica pointed toward a door. "There's a bathroom in there if you need one. And over there," she said, then pointed toward another door, "that door leads to David's office. Please don't interrupt him."

She smiled politely as she talked, but there was no mistaking her impersonal manner. Her unspoken warning wasn't lost on Tanya. The woman didn't like her, and she had to wonder why. Could she and David have had a relationship in the past? "There's reading material on the table," she informed her. "If you'd like a cup of coffee or a drink, please help yourself."

Walking across the room, she pushed a button that was practically invisible on the wall casing. Two doors Tanya hadn't noticed earlier opened, disappearing into the walls, revealing a well-stocked bar. Tanya couldn't help but wonder at Jessica's casual manner as she moved through the room. Did she know it so well because she and David had shared stolen moments here together?

The thought of David with this woman made her stomach churn. Not wanting to clue Jessica in to what she was thinking, she carefully kept her emotions under control. "I'm fine," Tanya replied, ready to be left alone.

Jessica walked to the desk. "If you need anything, just press the intercom," she instructed, pointing to the phone on the table.

Tanya watched her leave. She strolled through the room with curiosity, seeking any opportunity, however slight, to catch a glimpse into David's life in Atlanta.

There was little there to analyze. The perfectly kept bathroom held no clues at all. She heard his muffled voice in the next room, his words indistinguishable as he spoke with Justin.

She'd been surprised, again, by the size of his company. There had to have been at least thirty employees working for him in his office. The sense of anxiety that she'd felt upon arriving in Atlanta became stronger. David belonged here in Atlanta, not at Cottonwood. Although they'd begun a relationship, she figured it was futile for her to believe that anything permanent could come of it.

David was sticking out his time at the plantation because he had to. Their intimacy hadn't changed anything, and sadly, it never would. Discouraged, she took a seat on the sofa, picked up a magazine and began to thumb through it.

After about thirty minutes of waiting, she heard the door that led to David's office open, and Justin came into the room.

"Hello. I guess you're about bored out of your mind by now, right?"

She smiled at him. "I didn't mind waiting."

"Well, David is with Delgado now, and I'm in charge of you. If you're ready, I'll take you to your appointment."

Tanya picked up her purse and followed him. Together they walked to his car, Justin making an effort to put her at ease. "David should be free by dinnertime. He's going to be tied up longer that we'd planned."

"That's all right. I know your time is important. I could have caught a cab or something." From what Tanya had observed, besides being friends, the two men shared a mutual respect for each other.

He shot her a skeptical look as he parked at the doctor's office. "You're kidding, right? I've got orders not to let you out of my sight."

Surprised, her eyes met his. "I'm perfectly capable of taking care of myself."

"I'm sure you are. But I'm only following David's orders."

Before she could stop herself, she asked, "Do you normally entertain women for him?"

"Hardly," he countered, flashing an engaging grin. "The man works all the time. He doesn't have a life. I can't count the number of times I've tried to set him up with someone, but he always finds an excuse not to accept."

"Oh."

"I'm not saying he's been a monk," he clarified. "But

I've never seen him get involved with a woman, not like he is with you."

Tanya flushed to her roots. "We're not involved," she quickly clarified.

"If you say so," Justin answered, but it was clear he was skeptical.

She felt compelled to make him believe her. "We're not."

"Okay." Justin took her arm.

She didn't miss the way his eyes twinkled. "You don't believe me." Not wanting to admit to an intimate relationship, there was little she could say. But with Justin's words, her worst fears had been confirmed.

David didn't get involved with women.

Not emotionally.

Not even with her.

Nine

"**H**ere she is. Delivered back in perfect condition, just like I promised," Justin announced. They'd just arrived back at David's office, having been gone nearly the entire day.

Tanya glared playfully at Justin. "Thank you, I think." She touched his arm fondly. During the time she'd spent with him this afternoon, she'd gotten to know David's friend better. He was as nice as he was handsome.

"It was my pleasure, ma'am," he replied with a wink.

David listened to the banter between Tanya and Justin without amusement, his attention centered on Tanya's hand lying on Justin's arm. Maybe he shouldn't have asked his friend to take care of her. It appeared as if they were getting along just a little *too* well. He pulled at the collar of his dress shirt. What had he been thinking, pairing those two up? Justin had no trouble when it came to attracting women.

In the privacy of his office, David rounded on them. "Where in hell have you been?" He checked his watch. "It's been six hours since you left!"

Justin's eyebrows rose at David's curt tone. "Well, hell, we went for a few drinks, then decided to have some fun and spent the whole afternoon dancing," Justin answered, his expression bland.

"Cute." But David didn't find his friend's comment at all humorous. Though he'd known where they were, he'd had a hard time keeping his mind on his work. Okay, he'd missed Tanya. Dammit, he hadn't expected to feel this way about her—like being without her was eating him up inside.

"Where do you think we've been? Lucas saw Tanya right away, but then he sent her for tests, which took all afternoon."

Looking apologetic, Tanya said to Justin, "I'm really sorry it took so long and tied up your day."

He took her hand. "Not a problem." His gaze went to David. "She's been a champ putting up with all of it." Nodding toward David's desk, with stacks of papers spread on it, he added, "I'm surprised you noticed. Looks like you've been busy."

"What did Lucas say?" David asked, scowling at Justin's casualness with Tanya. He got up and walked around the desk, stopping before them. It took every ounce of his control not to warn Justin to back off.

Reeling from David's reaction to her and Justin being out together, Tanya fielded his question. "He said it was possible that my memory was returning, but right now there's just no way to be sure." Her examination had taken longer than Tanya had anticipated, but she'd appreciated Dr. Avery's thoroughness.

"Lucas pulled some strings and sent her to a diagnostic center for some tests. I don't know how he managed it, but he had the results by the time we returned to his office." Justin took a seat on the sofa, then sat back and stretched out his legs.

"What did the tests indicate?" David asked, eager to know what she'd found out. Disappointed, Tanya sighed. She'd been hoping to learn something that would medically confirm that she was regaining her memory. "Very little, I'm afraid. Dr. Avery didn't have the results of the tests I'd had years ago to compare them with. The good news is that he didn't see anything to indicate any problems."

"Is he sending for the results of your earlier tests?"

She nodded. "It'll be a few days before he gets them, after the holiday. He said he'd call me."

"And in the meantime?" David had suspected that Lucas wouldn't be able to tell them anything definite, but he'd played it safe by insisting that Tanya be examined. He'd wanted to be sure that there wasn't some delayed trauma from her head injury. He breathed a sigh of relief. His biggest fear was that she had some kind of tumor, causing the strange and unexplainable dreams that plagued her.

"He told me not to force myself to remember. To do so could be dangerous. If my memory is returning, I should let it come naturally." Despite the doctor's advice, how could she relax? She was convinced she was remembering her past. As excited as she was about it, she was frightened, as well.

Would she like the person she used to be? Or would she be ashamed of who she had been?

"Sounds like reasonable advice," David commented.

"If it was happening to you, you wouldn't think that. I'm going crazy wondering what's happening. I want answers. If my memory is returning—"

David took her hand, his expression filled with compassion. "You've got a point. But please try to do as he says. It may make your memory return faster if you try not to push yourself, if you just let it come back at its own pace." He glanced at his watch. "Are you ready for dinner? I'm finished for the day." His gaze went to Justin. "Delgado is on board. He'll be in touch with you in the morning."

Tanya gasped. They hadn't had time to stop for lunch. "Oh my, I didn't even think about lunch," she apologized to Justin. "You must be starving."

Justin stood. "As a matter of fact, I am. Where are we going?"

"Tanya and I are going to dinner at Nikolai's Roof," he said, naming one of the most upscale restaurants in Atlanta that specialized in Russian cuisine. "I don't know where you're going."

"David!" Tanya chastised, appalled.

Holding his hands up, Justin retorted, "That's okay. I know when I'm not wanted."

"We'd love to have you join us, wouldn't we?" she insisted, ignoring the flare of irritation in David's eyes. Justin had spent the entire day taking care of her. The least David could do was show his gratitude.

"No, no, that's okay." Moving closer, Justin chuckled and took her hand. "Actually, I have plans tonight. I was just harassing this guy," he admitted. "I enjoyed spending the day with you. I have a feeling I'll be seeing more of you." Then, as if to stoke David's annoyance, he leaned close and kissed her cheek.

Smiling, Tanya watched him leave. When Justin closed the door behind him, she confronted David. "That was rude."

"Why? Because I wanted you to myself? Believe me, Justin knew exactly what he was doing."

She crossed her arms in front of her. "Which was what?" She couldn't wait to hear this.

"Justin thought he was being amusing inviting himself along."

"I thought he was just being friendly."

"He knew I wanted to be alone with you."

"Oh." Tanya's heart tripped over itself at the possessive look in David's eyes. She didn't resist when he tugged her to him. "To do what?" she asked, her voice husky.

"This." His lips came down on hers. He ran the tip of his tongue around her teeth, then deepened the kiss, angling his mouth on hers. Her arms went around his neck and she moved closer, pressing herself against him.

His hand found her breast. With a moan, she broke off the kiss. "I don't think this is a good idea." But even as she said the words, she boldly slid her hand below his waist and stroked him through his slacks. He was hard, and knowing she could do that to him with just a kiss sent a wave of desire through her. "Someone could come in at any moment," she whispered against his mouth as he continued kissing her.

Of course, she thought with a touch of arrogance, if it was Jessica, she wouldn't mind so much. She wanted the woman to know that David wasn't available.

"I'm the boss," he told her, kissing his way down her

throat. "No one will come in. We'll go into the other room and lock the door."

"Your assistant has a key to that room," Tanya said, remembering when Jessica had taken it from her desk. Still, she arched her back as he unbuttoned her blouse and ran his tongue along the edge of her bra.

"She won't use it." He stopped long enough to take her hand and tug her into the small room off of his office. "Besides, it's getting late. Everyone will be leaving soon." After shutting the door and locking it, he backed her toward the sofa. His mouth came down on hers, drinking her in.

"She has a thing for you, you know," Tanya said, lifting her lips from his.

David stopped in the process of unfastening her bra, leaving it hanging loosely around her breasts. "What?"

"Jessica," she said, her tone sharper than she had intended. "She wants you."

His mouth quirked up as he loosened his tie and removed his shirt. What Tanya was suggesting wasn't true. He'd known Jessica for a long time, and he knew she prided herself on guarding his time. Maybe Tanya had mistaken his assistant's protective manner for something else entirely. Jessica was a striking woman, but he wasn't attracted to her, never had been. "What makes you think that?" The spark of jealousy in Tanya's eyes pleased him.

Tanya watched him undress and gasped when he began unbuckling his belt. "Well, for one thing, she was very distant to me when she brought me in here."

He brushed her mouth with his. "Oh," he answered, his tone making it sound as if what she'd said made no sense at all.

"And I've seen the way she looks at you." She

frowned at his amused expression. "I'm not kidding." Leaning back, she stared into his eyes. "Has she been here with you before?"

After slipping her blouse from her shoulders, he removed her bra, leaving her standing half-naked in front of him. Unable to resist, he touched her breast, then stroked her nipple with his thumb. "You mean like this?" he asked softly.

Tanya nodded and a lump formed in her throat. It was logical that he'd known other women before her, but she just couldn't stand the idea of making love with him in that room if he'd been intimate there with someone else.

He bent down and took her breast into his mouth, sucking it gently before straightening and looking into her eyes. "What if she has?" he asked bluntly. "Would you be jealous?" As he waited for her answer, he molded her breasts with his hands.

She swallowed hard. "Yes," she admitted quietly, then her lids lowered slightly as she began to succumb to the intense pleasure of his touch.

Though her reply was everything he'd hoped for, her admission floored him. David met her gaze. "I've never been intimate with her here or anyplace else." Pulling Tanya against him, he whispered, "You're the woman I want. Right here. Right now."

Forever his mind whispered, but he couldn't bring himself to say the word out loud. He couldn't take the chance and admit that she was all he'd thought about, that she was the only woman he ever wanted.

If he did, and she ever walked away, he'd be devastated. He couldn't allow himself to fall in love with her.

Driven by desire, he lowered her to the sofa and

stroked her body as he kissed her mouth. He unfastened her slacks and slid them down her thighs, removing them along with her shoes as he kissed her belly. His fingers brushed dangerously close to the most sensitive part of her body, and her hips moved against them.

Tanya moaned with pleasure. He wanted her.

Only her.

Hearing him admit his feelings gave her hope that one day he'd feel something more for her. That feeling of foreboding she'd had when she'd first arrived disappeared as her hopes escalated. Maybe one day he would love her.

Maybe he already did and he didn't even know it.

He caressed her between her legs, and she gasped, forgetting everything except the erotic explosion his touch ignited. The experience of him touching her so intimately stole her breath. She bit her lip to stop herself from crying out. "Please, David, please, make love to me," she whispered.

David shed his pants and shoes, then eased himself over her. She opened her thighs to him, and he thrust himself deep inside of her. He groaned as she took him, her hips moving in rhythm with his. With a sense of awareness he'd never experienced before, he watched her, how her eyes filled with rapture as he quickened the rhythm of their lovemaking. How her breath came in harsh pants, and how, with each stroke, she tightened her arms around him. When she cried out, he covered her mouth and swallowed the sound of her moans as she reached the peak of ecstasy. He thrust faster and harder, burying himself inside her. At his own release, he admitted the truth to himself. He'd done more than just make love to her.

He'd allowed himself to fall in love with her.

* * *

The phone rang. As she reached for the extension on the nightstand, Tanya yawned and opened her eyes. "Hello?" She was surprised when she recognized the voice on the line. "Oh, hi, Justin. Hold on for just a moment, and I'll get him." She didn't have to go far. David was lying right beside her, in his bed, in his Atlanta apartment.

She rolled over to wake him, but when she looked at his face, she found him watching her. Her heart melted. With each moment they spent together, her love for him was growing stronger. And she was powerless to stop it.

"Good morning," she murmured with a smile. "It's for you."

David took the phone from her, but before he answered it, he leaned over and kissed her neck as his hand slid to her breast.

Closing her eyes, Tanya moaned softly, then realized that she'd forgotten the phone. "Stop it!" she whispered. Her face reddened, but her body thrummed with pure pleasure under his sensual touch.

David infuriated her further by chuckling. Then he whispered, "Go back to sleep. I'll take it downstairs." Balancing the phone with his shoulder, he slipped into the slacks he'd taken off the previous night, then zipped them as he walked barefoot out of the room.

Tanya lay on her side and watched him disappear through the door. After making love with him in his office, they'd come to his condo to shower and change their clothes. David had taken her out to dinner, then they'd returned to his place, where they'd spent the rest of the evening in bed.

As David had assured her, by the time they'd left the

office, everyone else had gone, including Jessica. Even though David had said that no would disturb them, Tanya was sure that his assistant had known *exactly* what they were doing behind those locked doors.

She blushed just thinking about how they'd made love in David's office as she glanced around his bedroom. Located near his work, his home was in a high-rise complex. His condo was classy, roomy and surprisingly comfortable. Spacious rooms and luxurious furnishings filled his apartment. The bathroom, with a spa tub and separate shower, was larger than ones she'd seen in fancy homes on television.

Still, the entire apartment lacked the coziness that always offered her comfort at the plantation. That David considered Atlanta his home and felt perfectly comfortable here in this apartment spoke volumes about him. He was used to the finer things in life, not the hard, physical work of the plantation.

Her stomach growled. Rather than wait for him to come back to bed, she got up, thinking she'd make them breakfast while he was on the telephone. Spotting his shirt, she slipped it on and buttoned it up. It covered her to the tops of her thighs, and she felt presentable enough to move around the house.

She was walking down the hall when she heard David's voice. Realizing that he was on the phone in the kitchen, she stopped in the hall, not wanting to interrupt him. Though she hadn't intended on listening to his conversation, when she heard him mention Cottonwood, she stilled. Her curiosity kept her feet planted to the floor. David's voice was clear and terse as he spoke to Justin.

"Because I have no choice." After a few moments of

silence, he spoke again, this time his voice lower and much more succinct. "I made that clear from the start. My plans haven't changed."

Tanya's breath got trapped in her lungs.

Because I have no choice.

She'd known all along that David was staying at Cottonwood out of necessity, not because he wanted to be there. Why had she let herself believe a week had changed anything?

I made that clear from the start. My plans haven't changed.

Dizziness overcame her as she struggled to make her way back to the bedroom. She was a fool. Though she'd told herself that he could change, that maybe one day he would grow to love the plantation and want to make it his home, she'd been wrong. His feelings for Cottonwood went only as deep as his desire to keep the plantation in his family.

And his feelings for her? Her gaze fell on the rumpled bed. He desired her. Pure and simple, he desired her. And he'd never once led her to believe anything permanent would come from their relationship. If she'd hoped David would fall in love with her, she needed to face reality. That wasn't going to happen.

On the verge of tears, Tanya sat on the edge of the bed, her heart aching. Would his desire for her be enough for her to live with? She'd loved him practically from the moment she'd first seen him, when she'd been a lost teenager trying to find her way in a new and scary place.

All those years ago, when he'd walked away from her, she'd been hurt, but it had been the kind of misery she'd been able to live with. Could she spend the next year making love with him, knowing in her heart that he would be leaving her and returning to his life here in Atlanta?

Before she could think of what she should do, David strolled back into the room. Glancing at him, she swallowed past the lump in her throat and found the courage to speak. "Is everything all right? Do you have to go to the office?"

David's gaze drifted over her, noticing the tightness in her features. He was beginning to recognize her moods, knew when she was angry or worried or sad. He wondered if something had upset her in the few minutes he'd been on the phone. But he couldn't think of what. "No. Justin's going to take care of what I needed to do this morning." At her frown, he asked, "Are you okay?"

She gave him a smile that didn't quite make it to her eyes. "I'm fine. I guess I should shower and change so we can pack."

He didn't miss the catch in her voice when she spoke. Something was definitely wrong. "There's no rush. We have plenty of time. Thanksgiving isn't until tomorrow."

Avoiding his gaze, Tanya stood and gathered some clothes to take into the bathroom. "I know, but I'm anxious to go home."

"You sure you're okay?" Despite her assurances, he didn't miss the trace of tears in her eyes. Massaging her shoulder with his hand, he asked, "Did you have a bad dream after I got up?"

Tanya forced herself to meet his gaze. "Yes," she lied. It was then that she realized she hadn't had a dream last night. How strange, she thought. She'd begun to believe that her memory could be returning, and last night she hadn't had even a hint of a dream.

"Do you want to talk about it?"

"What?" She looked at him, her expression perplexed. "Um, no." Stepping away, she disengaged herself from him. "I'm okay. Just a bit shaken." That was the truth. It just didn't have anything to do with a dream.

"Go ahead and shower, then. Maybe you'll feel better."

Tanya took a quick shower, anxious to get home, where she could be by herself. She needed to think about what, if anything, she should do about her relationship with David. When she came back into the room, she was practically dressed. "Your turn," she said, making an effort to keep her voice even.

David headed for the bathroom, then stopped beside her and kissed her. Her eyelids drifted shut as his mouth moved on hers. Despite the warning to her heart, she slipped her hands up to his chest and sank into his kiss, greedy for every moment she could have with him. She'd known she was taking a risk when she'd become involved with David. He put his arms around her and drew her tighter against his body. Heat flared quickly inside her, ignited by his nearness, by his mouth possessing hers.

"You smell wonderful," he rasped, and his mouth moved to her throat.

"David," she whispered, knowing that if she didn't stop kissing him, they'd end up in bed. She placed her hands against his chest, could feel the rapid beat of his heart. "Your shower," she prompted, her breathing uneven. "We need to leave shortly."

"I know," he said, then kissed her mouth again.

When he lifted his head, she licked her lips, tasting him, and it made her want him even more. Still, she wanted to go home. To Cottonwood. Where she felt safe. "I'll be ready by the time you're finished."

He nodded, then stepped away and disappeared into the bathroom.

Tears stung her eyes as she began packing her clothes. What was she going to do? What could she do? She loved him. But she realized the hopelessness of her situation.

David didn't love her.

He never would.

Ten

Holding back the curtain, Tanya stared out the dining room window at the bare trees that lined the long driveway to the main house. Paralleling her gloomy mood, Thanksgiving Day had arrived with a dark, overcast sky. A chill swept through her that had nothing to do with the crisp weather outside. She'd been looking forward to this day, to spending it with David. Now that it had arrived, she felt a vague sense of uneasiness, an anxiety that she couldn't explain. Lately, nothing in her life had gone right.

Well, that wasn't entirely true. She'd fulfilled her dream of being with David, of lying in his arms and making love with him.

But at what price? her mind whispered. *At the price of your heart?*

Yes. That was a done deal.

She clenched her bottom lip with her teeth and sighed, wishing with all her heart that he loved her as well. Though he'd been attentive and loving toward her since they'd arrived home, he'd never once whispered words of love to her.

Tanya knew better than to expect him to, but the yearning of her heart wasn't so easy to control. Though she knew that David had been hurt in the past, first by Edward, and later by his ex-fiancée, Melanie, she still wanted him to love her, to ask her to stay at Cottonwood with him forever.

And wasn't that the stuff fairy tales were made of? Wishes and dreams?

As she turned from the window, the painting hanging over the large, cherry buffet caught her attention. Edward had told her that, as a present for David's mother, he'd hired an artist to paint Cottonwood shortly after they'd married. The artist had perfectly caught the architecture of the house and grounds, painting it in warm hues of color, capturing its soul in a hauntingly still image.

Everything she loved about it.

But no matter how she felt about this house, David could never be happy here. She knew that now. For him, there were too many unhappy memories, memories he seemed unable to let go.

Even for her.

She really couldn't blame him; she even understood why. As a child, he'd felt rejected by his father, and he'd never recovered from it.

She'd seen how dynamic and intense he could be when discussing a business deal with Justin or on a telephone conference with a client.

That man was the real David Taylor. Atlanta was the

life he'd yearned for when he'd left here. He'd worked hard to build a lucrative business. He was doing what he was meant to do.

David had never planned on returning to Cottonwood or being forced to live here. His feelings for her hadn't altered his plans.

Their affair had only complicated things between them. No matter how much it hurt her, she had to face that simple truth—she would have to leave Cottonwood. She couldn't live here with him, not without continuing their relationship. And continuing to live here with him, making love with him, would only cause her more pain in the end. The longer she stayed, the harder it would be when he walked away and returned to Atlanta.

She drew in a deep breath. Having made the decision to leave, peace enveloped her, an inner calm that had eluded her since returning from Atlanta. It would be hard to go, but in the long run, her heartache would be easier to live with if she wasn't living at Cottonwood. Though Edward's will stipulated that she could work here as long as she wanted, if she left, David would immediately inherit the plantation.

Which was what he'd always wanted.

At the sound of footsteps, Tanya moved away from the window. Her heart ached at the sight of David as he came into the room.

She forced a smile to her lips as their eyes met. "Hi."

David pulled her into his arms. "Hi, yourself." He kissed her mouth hungrily, then leaned away and examined her face. "You okay?" Not for the first time, he wondered what she had been thinking since they'd left Atlanta. Upon arriving home, she'd been unusually quiet. Something was bothering her. Whenever he'd asked what was troubling her, she'd quickly denied anything was wrong, leading him to believe he had no reason to worry.

Until he saw her again. The inherent sadness in her eyes prompted his concern, and his doubts resurfaced.

"I'm fine. Are you ready to go? The celebration should be about ready to get underway."

Excited about sharing Cotton Creek's Thanksgiving celebration with her, David picked up her jacket from the coat tree as they walked into the foyer. He remembered the fun times he'd shared with his parents when he'd gone to the festival as a child. After his mother had died, he'd gone alone or with a friend.

Never with his father.

Thinking of his father failed to spoil David's anticipation of going to the celebration with Tanya. That surprised him. Now he was able to remember the good times with his father without feeling the pain and rejection that had kept him away from home.

"You might need this," he said, and helped her slip on her coat. "The temperature's dropped outside. I think a cold front moved through this morning." With the mention of the cooler temperature, David found himself thinking about being at Cottonwood during the winter months, spending even more time with Tanya. Snuggling up to a warm fire. Making love to her.

The late afternoon air was cool as they got into his car. Minutes later, as they arrived at the edge of the small town, music spilled out from the festival area.

"I think that's a high school band," she said as David pulled to the curb on one of the side streets and parked.

"They sound pretty good." He was out of the car and rounding the front as Tanya opened her door.

They made their way behind a row of buildings toward the music.

As they approached the celebration, a sensation of homecoming overwhelmed David. The festival, held in a large park located in the center of town, was hidden from view from the main streets. Balloons and streamers hung from the many trees. Food vendors lined the outer edges of the park, and a crowd had already gathered throughout the area. A temporary stage had been set up in the center of the park for a band to perform prior to the fireworks that would conclude the evening.

Surprisingly, little about the town and park had changed since David's last visit. The trees were taller and some of the faces were different due to the town's increased population. Excitement pulsed through the crowd walking along the winding sidewalks.

For the first time in what seemed like a century, David felt as if he belonged in Cotton Creek. Coming home hadn't been as difficult as he'd once thought it would be since he'd dealt with his father's death. Was it possible that he could put his feelings for his father completely to rest and make Cottonwood his home again?

Because of Tanya?

The thought didn't scare him as it once would have. He could see himself living here, strolling through the park with Tanya, their kids romping in the playground. The possibility of sharing the rest of his life with her filled an emptiness inside him that had haunted him for years.

That he could even think of living here was remarkable. Because he'd been trying to prove to his father that he was a success for so long, he'd forgotten how to just enjoy life. The value of his roots.

And he had them here. They grew deep. Generations of his ancestors had made Cottonwood Plantation their home.

Memories of his mother were here, memories he cherished. How could he have ever believed that he could stay away?

As they meandered through the growing crowd of people, David tightened his hold on Tanya's hand, interlacing their fingers. Stopping every now and then, they spoke to friends and acquaintances. He even reminisced with a few of the people he'd known in high school.

Tanya spotted a vendor selling cotton candy and she practically squealed. "You can buy it in the store now, in a bag, did you know that?" she asked, her eyes filled with excitement as she dragged him to the line. "But it isn't nearly as good as getting it made right in front of you."

David chuckled, then fished in his pocket for money. "It doesn't take much to make you happy, does it?" he asked as he paid the vendor, then handed Tanya the cotton candy.

Only your love, Tanya's mind whispered. But she already knew that was too much to ask for. She forced herself not to think about the decision she'd made to leave, wanting only to cherish each moment she had with David. Sticking her tongue out at him, she started to turn and walk to the stand where the high school band was playing, but was halted abruptly as David pulled her to him for a kiss.

"You taste like cherries and sugar."

She grinned. "Are you complaining?"

"No, but I want to do a lot more than just taste you." With a grin, he kissed her again, a drugging, sensual bonding of their mouths that made him want to touch her in places not allowed in public.

Tanya moaned softly as she broke away and stepped back, smiling at him. "Want some?" she asked, then before he could answer, she stuffed a gob of the sugary mass into his mouth. "Isn't it—"

"Oh, my God! Victoria?"

Tanya started, and a chill raced down her spine. Unsure why, she shrugged off the uneasy feeling, then glanced at the woman who had spoken to her. There was a man with her, someone she was sure she'd never seen.

The woman, well, Tanya wasn't so sure. She didn't recognize her, but there was something about her that seemed…familiar. Her eyes were wide with shock, her mouth hung open as she stared back. She seemed genuinely startled, and obviously she thought she was someone Tanya knew. "No, I'm sorry. You must have me confused with someone else." Smiling politely, Tanya turned and started to walk away.

"No! Wait!"

Grabbing her arm, the woman stopped Tanya. Every muscle in Tanya's body tensed. She turned to face her again, and the uneasy feeling inside her escalated, frightening her. "Yes?"

"Victoria, it's Imogene!" the woman cried.

Tanya stared at her, wondering what she should say. Obviously, this lady thought she knew her. But no matter how hard she tried, Tanya couldn't recall meeting her. "I told you, my name isn't Victoria. It's Tanya, Tanya Winters." But even as she said the words, a sensation that she'd seen the woman before overwhelmed her. Her pulse began to race. "Perhaps we've met before, but I'm sorry, I just can't place you."

Her gaze slid over the woman, her mind searching for some recollection of where they might have met.

Only a few years older than herself, the woman's chin-length blond hair framed her pretty face. And there was something intriguing in her striking green eyes. They were incredulous, drawing Tanya in.

Tanya drew in a sharp breath as the full impact of the woman's statement hit her. The woman *believed* that she was someone named Victoria.

The man with her, well, if Tanya had met him before, there was no way she would have forgotten him. Tall and handsome, his raven hair was a stark contrast to his intense gray eyes. No, she was sure she'd never seen him.

"Look," David interjected, concerned that the stranger hadn't let Tanya go. "Obviously she looks like—"

"No, please give me a minute," the woman implored, her voice gentle but insistent, her gaze fierce. "Please, listen to me. I'm not mistaken." She glanced briefly at her companion, as if appealing for his help, then back to them. "Look," she said, seeming to take a moment to calm herself. "My name is Imogene Shakir. This is my husband, Raf. My maiden name is Danforth." As if she expected Tanya to recognize her name, she stopped speaking and waited.

Suddenly very anxious, Tanya shook free from the woman and moved closer to David. He slipped his arm around her. "Danforth? Are you related to Senator Danforth?" David asked.

Imogene Shakir nodded, and her eyes began to water. "Yes. Yes, I am. He's my uncle."

"Oh." Tanya wasn't sure what else to say. The woman looked as if she was going to cry.

"He's *our* uncle."

Tanya frowned, not really understanding what she was talking about. "No, I'm sorry. You have me confused with someone else." But she couldn't ignore the tears forming in the woman's eyes, or the distressed, yet determined look on her face.

Imogene very slowly reached toward her again, grasping her arm even more forcefully this time. "You're my sister. Your name is Victoria. I know you think I'm crazy, but I'm not." She spoke a little faster, with an urgency in her voice. "Five years ago, you left home with a friend to attend a rock concert in Atlanta. As a birthday present, our brother Jake bought tickets for you and I to go together. But I wasn't able to go, so you invited a girl, a new friend of yours, to go with you. *Her* name was Tanya Winters. You are my sister, Victoria Danforth. You disappeared after the concert. We've been searching for you all this time."

Tanya could feel the woman shaking. It vibrated through her own body. Her gaze sought David's. He was looking at her with a strange expression on his face. Dazed, she bent her head and put her hands over her face. Something flashed through her mind, a myriad of faces and settings, each moving so rapidly that she couldn't make them out clearly before they disappeared.

"I—I don't know." Looking back at them, Tanya stared speechless at the couple.

"It is true," Raf Shakir said. "I have seen your pictures."

David held her tighter. "Tanya?"

"Think, Victoria," Imogene implored, her voice rising. "It was the day of your seventeenth birthday. There was a big bash that day. Mom and Dad had a party with all of our family right before you left. I was supposed to go to the concert with you. Not Tanya Winters."

Swallowing past the knot in her throat, Tanya's disconcerted gaze went from the woman's face to David's.

A sharp pain stabbed her in her temple as another series of images blazed through her mind. "Oh, my God. Oh, my God." She began to shake so hard that she couldn't breathe.

"Tori?" Imogene called out, and her eyes filled with hope.

Suddenly everything racing through Tanya's mind stopped. She saw an image of herself and the woman standing in front of her. They were younger, just teenagers, and they were in a bedroom, sitting on a bed, laughing. She shook her head. In a blink, the image disappeared, replaced by one of herself standing in a grand house with people all around her. There were balloons, and candles on a beautiful two-tiered cake with the name *Victoria* written in pink on it.

Blood roared through her head. Her ears began to pound. Everything around her began to blur. Tanya looked at Imogene, squinting through tears that were now streaming down her cheeks.

"Genie?" she whispered, then she fell into a black void.

David caught Victoria as her body went slack, and he eased her to the ground. His heart in his throat, he dropped down to his knees and held her while he tried to awaken her. He gently patted her face with his palm. "Tanya! Sweetheart. I'm here with you. Come on, Tanya." She moaned, then looked at him briefly before her eyes closed again. "Tanya, honey, look at me."

Her eyelids floated open, but her pupils remained dilated and unfocused. "David?" Her voice came out a breathless whisper.

A crowd had gathered around them. David could hear them whispering, knew they'd overheard some of their conversation. His gaze shot to the woman and man also kneeling on the ground beside Tanya. "She may be going into shock."

Someone shouted that they were calling 911. David ignored them. "I'm taking her to the hospital," he said to Imogene. "It'll be faster than waiting for the paramedics."

"Of course. We'll go along," Imogene said, her tone kind but firm.

"We'll drive you." Raf already had his keys in his hand.

David hesitated a moment, thinking about his options.

"We arrived early and our car is parked right along the curb in front of this building. You'll want to hold her."

The two men exchanged a knowing look, and David gave a quick nod. Despite what they'd said, that Tanya was really Victoria Danforth, Imogene's sister, David wasn't giving any margin of access to her until he knew what the hell was going on.

David paced the waiting room of the hospital like a caged animal. Upon arriving there with Imogene and Raf Shakir, he'd been met by a nurse. He gave her a brief rundown of what had happened in the park, and they ushered Tanya into one of the treatment rooms.

As they'd begun to examine her, David had explained what had happened in the park to the attending doctor. He also informed him about the pertinent details of her past, of her strange dreams, her persistent headaches and her familiarity with places she'd thought she'd never been. Despite his protests, he'd been ushered into a waiting room and forced to leave Tanya in the doctor's care.

Was Tanya really Victoria Danforth, the niece of Senator Abraham Danforth, the young girl who had disappeared five years ago?

His mind reeled from the significance of his thoughts. He couldn't believe it, yet in a strange way, it made perfect sense. She walked with a natural grace, something he'd noticed often, most recently in the way she'd handled herself in D.C. And in spite of what they'd believed was her background, a troubled teen with no family support, she was self-reliant and confident. Though she hadn't known who she was, her character strengths and her well-bred upbringing had shone through.

And those dreams of people that she thought she knew. Were they another clue to her identity? What about the feeling that she'd recognized places without ever remembering being there?

"She'll be all right," Imogene whispered, coming up beside David and placing her hand gently on his arm. She gave him a reassuring squeeze.

David turned and looked at Imogene Danforth Shakir. Her hair was blond, like Tanya's, but Imogene's was cut short, in a style that set off her green eyes. "Will she?" he asked quietly, wanting to believe her. Frustrated, he rubbed his face with his hand. "She's been through so much."

"I know this was a shock, but I have to believe it was meant to be that I found her. My family has never given up hope of finding Tori." She bit her lip, her expression one of open curiosity. "I don't mean to be forward, but who are you?"

"My name is David Taylor. I've known Tanya for the past five years, but in the past couple of weeks we've become…reacquainted." He could think of no other way to describe their relationship that wouldn't add suspicion to the concern in Imogene's eyes.

"Has she lived with you for the past five years?" she asked. "In Cotton Creek?"

"No," he answered. "Not with me. With my father, Edward Taylor, on our family plantation. It's just outside of town. He recently passed away, but he took Tanya in five years ago when she had no home, no family to care for her."

"Victoria," she corrected him, then her gaze softened. "I'm sorry about your father." He nodded his thanks, but when he remained silent, she asked, "How did he come to know Victoria?"

"After she'd recovered from her injury, she was set to go into a group home. When my father heard about her situation, he took her on as an intern and offered her a job and a place to live."

"Injury?" Imogene's eyes widened. "What kind of injury?"

"Apparently, she suffered a concussion. No one knows what happened to her. All we were told is that she was found unconscious by the side of the road. When she awoke, she couldn't remember anything."

Imogene raised a hand to her throat. "Oh, my God!" she exclaimed. "She didn't remember anything?"

David shook his head. "She's had amnesia ever since."

Raf slipped a protective arm around his wife's shoulders. "That is all over now. We must be happy that we've found her and she's safe."

"You're right, Raf, of course." She turned to David. "But what happened to her? Was she hurt in any other way?" she asked, her voice shaking. "Was she—"

"No," David said quickly, wanting to assure Imogene that Tanya hadn't been sexually abused. "Other than a concussion and losing her memory, she showed no other signs of being harmed." His mouth tightened a fraction.

He didn't elaborate on his answer. He wasn't about to admit that he'd been the first man to make love to her.

And he wanted to be the last.

He loved her.

Hell, he'd loved her from the first moment he'd seen her. Except at the time, he'd been too damned angry at his father to let anyone near him. And he'd held on to that anger for years, staying away from Cottonwood, away from Tanya.

From *Victoria*.

He fixed Imogene with a hard stare. "You're absolutely positive that she's your sister?"

"Yes." She looked around her, then spotted her purse on a chair. "Wait." Rushing across the room, she dug into her purse. She withdrew her wallet and flipped it open to a picture. Returning to David, she held it out in front of him. "This is Victoria when she was seventeen. It was taken on her birthday, the day she disappeared. I've carried it with me ever since. I've never given up hope of finding her."

One glance at the picture and David knew.

Tanya *was* Victoria Danforth.

Her resemblance to the girl in the photo was uncanny. "She's been having a lot of disturbing dreams lately. As a matter of fact, she was just examined by a specialist a few days ago in Atlanta, a friend of mine. Tanya and I suspected that her memory was returning. The shock of seeing you must have broken the final barrier of her amnesia."

Imogene paled. "I had a dream about Victoria, too. She was in a field on our horse farm, and every time I tried to reach her, she disappeared."

Shaking his head, David's gaze locked with Imogene's. He could see the resemblance between the two women. "I've always known her as Tanya. Calling her Victoria is going to sound odd for a while."

A kind, understanding smile spread on her lips. "Then why don't you call her Tori. That's what we called—" she stopped, realizing what she'd said, then corrected herself, "It's what we call her."

"Tori," he repeated, testing the sound of her name as he said it. For some unexplainable reason, it felt right.

Taking a breath, Imogene informed him, "I think you should know that I've already called my parents. They were overjoyed, to say the least. And tremendously relieved. We all are."

"That's understandable." He glanced out the window to the street that ran alongside the hospital.

"I promised them I wouldn't let Victoria out of my sight. They're on their way here now to see her. They should arrive within the next couple of hours."

David wasn't surprised. Tori's parents would need to see her. And the Danforths were prominent people. Once the news leaked out that their missing daughter had been found, the hospital, along with this town, would erupt in chaos. The news media was going to feed on this story until the public was sick of hearing of it.

Damn, he'd been such a fool. He should have been more honest with himself and with Tori about his feelings for her. He should have told her how much he loved her.

Now he was afraid that he would never get the chance.

Eleven

A commotion near the entrance of the hospital caught David's attention. Several men and women were gathered there, their voices raised, all trying to speak at once. He surveyed the boisterous crowd, then glanced out the window to the parking lot. Various media trucks were parked outside the hospital with their antennas raised, several from the national networks. Then he understood. The crowd of people rushing the reception desk were reporters eager for a story.

The news that the heiress, Victoria Danforth, had been found was out. Someone must have leaked the information to the press.

Great. This was just what Tanya needed. She hadn't had the time to come to grips with recovering her memory. The last thing she needed was a reporter trying to sneak into her room to take her picture.

Only she wasn't Tanya Winters, he reminded himself for the hundredth time since he'd arrived at the hospital. She was Victoria, and the paparazzi was ready and waiting to pounce on the smallest tidbit of information they could find out about her.

David's gaze went to the double doors separating him from Victoria. They'd been waiting over two hours, and it was killing him. He needed to know that she was all right.

The doors to the treatment area opened, and he rushed toward the doctor with whom he'd spoken earlier about Tori. Imogene and Raf were right on his heels as the older man in the white coat met them in the middle of the room.

"How is she?" David asked, his throat forming a knot as he waited for an update on her condition.

"She's doing okay." He glanced at the people congregated across the room and frowned. "Is that the news media?" he asked. Without waiting for an answer, he motioned for David, Imogene and Raf to follow him. "Under the circumstances, I think this will be more private," he said, leading them toward another room.

The crowd of people at the entrance noticed them and rushed in their direction. Two big doors closed behind them as they went into the treatment area, muting the voices of the paparazzi. The doctor led David, Imogene and Raf to a small, empty examination room.

"First, I want to assure you that Ms. Danforth is doing fine. I've checked her over thoroughly, and we've done several tests. After talking with her extensively, I believe her amnesia is completely gone." He shook his head. "Sometimes a head injury is like that. A person can have no recollection of their past, then with a snap, everything comes back."

"So she's all right?" Imogene asked, a tremble in her voice.

"She's anxious and feels quite overwhelmed. That's to be expected. From what you've told me, she's had a lot to endure today, as well as for the past five years. But, yes, she's doing well. Other than a slight headache, she has no complaints. She's handling the return of her memory with a lot of poise." He smiled. "It isn't hard to imagine that she came from a polished background."

"Will she have any relapses?"

"I don't believe so. It'll take a few days for her mind to comprehend everything and settle down. I'll give her a prescription for her headaches, but she may need only over-the-counter medication to treat them."

"Can I see her now?" David asked, and it sounded more like a demand.

"We want to see her, as well, doctor," Imogene added.

"Ms. Danforth wishes to see all of you, but I don't want her upset. She's composed herself, but it won't take very much to agitate her."

They followed the doctor across the hall, and as they started to go inside Victoria's room, the doctor stopped them. "I don't expect Ms. Danforth to have any further complications, but for the next few days, you should try to keep her from becoming too upset or anxious. She'll be free to leave once I sign her discharge papers. I would like for you to make sure that she has a follow-up visit with a specialist in a few days. Most importantly, she'll need to take it easy for a while."

David and Imogene nodded, and the doctor left them at the door to Victoria's room. Without waiting another moment, Imogene rushed inside, followed by Raf and then David. He wished he could have had a few minutes alone with Victoria. He wanted to talk to her, *needed* to talk to her, to tell her he loved her.

Circumstances, though, were not conducive to what *he* needed. Victoria had to come first. She was going to need time to adjust to the changes in her life—first and foremost, seeing her sister and learning about her family.

David hoped he wasn't going to lose her.

As he entered, his gaze settled immediately on Victoria. From her expression, he could tell that she was distressed, though she was struggling to hide it. Imogene hurried to her side, and David forced himself to stand back and give them privacy.

"Oh, Tori!" Tears brimmed in Imogene's eyes. "Sweetheart, are you okay?"

Victoria nodded. She was sitting up in the bed, dressed in a pale green hospital gown, a sheet pulled up to her waist. Her head felt as if an explosion had gone off inside it. Still struggling to get her bearings, she met her sister's gaze as Imogene stroked her arm. "Yes. I have a headache, but the doctor said that isn't unusual."

A headache, however bad, was the least of her concerns. For the first time in five years, she felt like somebody. Though she had lived as Tanya Winters, she'd never felt comfortable with the past that she'd assumed with the name.

She wasn't Tanya Winters, the girl from the streets. Everything that had happened to her was so clear now. It was as if it had happened so long ago, but then again, it felt like yesterday.

She wanted desperately to see her family, especially her mother and father. Oh, how she missed them. How were they? Had they been distraught when she disappeared? Had they blamed themselves? She needed to know that her parents were all right.

"We were so worried about you," Imogene was saying.

"I guess the shock of seeing you brought my memory back, sis," Victoria told her older sister. "How did you ever recognize me in that crowd?"

"I don't know. But earlier today I told Raf that we had to get back to the Thanksgiving celebration. I can't explain it, but there was an urgency that was steering me there." She glanced briefly at Raf, then met her sister's gaze. "Then I saw you. I was so scared. You wouldn't believe me when I told you that you were my sister."

Victoria chuckled, finding humor in the moment now that the tense situation had passed. "It was rather shocking. I keep hearing you saying my name over and over in my head." She squeezed her sister's hand. "Oh, Genie, I'm so glad you were persistent."

Tugging her sister closer, she reached up and ran her hand over Imogene's chic, short blond hair. "Goodness, let me look at you. I can't believe I've missed five years of your life. You're gorgeous."

Imogene hugged her sister fiercely, obviously making an effort not to cry. "Tori, honey, it's so good to have you back." She lost the battle with her tears and they spilled onto her cheeks. Dabbing at them, she sniffed, then blushed.

Squeezing her sister's hand, Victoria managed a smile. "I can't tell you how great it is to actually recognize you. It's even better knowing who I am." She cried too, then, but they were tears of sheer joy.

Stepping back a little, Imogene held her hand out to Raf. He came over and stood beside her. "This is my husband, Raf Shakir. We were recently married, and we live on a horse farm near Cotton Creek."

"Raf, it's so nice to meet you," Victoria said to the dynamic, dark-haired man beside Imogene as she brushed her tears away with her fingertips.

"Believe me, it is my pleasure," Raf assured her. "Genie has spoken of you often. You look very much like her. It is easy to believe that you are a Danforth. You are quite lovely."

Victoria smiled again, his sincerity and kindness assuring her that she would like Raf Shakir. And he loved her sister. She could see it in his eyes when he looked at Imogene.

"So that's why you were at the celebration?" Victoria asked, curious as to how her sister ended up at the town celebration. "Because you live nearby?" She frowned, her thoughts still a little confused. It was disconcerting to learn that her sister had lived so close to her, yet their paths had never crossed.

"Earlier today, we had attended Marc and Dana's wedding." Stopping herself when she realized that Victoria wasn't following, she briefly explained that their cousin, Marcus Danforth, had gotten married earlier in the day. Afterward, she and Raf had left before Thanksgiving dinner and the ensuing wedding festivities so they could return for the holiday celebration at Cotton Creek.

"This was our first year living in Cotton Creek together. Raf has lived here for some time," she explained. "We had promised some friends that we would meet them at the celebration." She gave a soft laugh as she looked at her husband. "They're probably wondering what happened to us."

Victoria's eyes filled with tears again, and she

sniffed. Her emotions were difficult to control. "Marc is married? God, Genie, this feels weird," she confessed. "I feel like I know you but I don't know you."

"Take it easy, honey," Imogene said. "Give it some time. The doctor told us that it would take a while before you feel oriented to your previous life. You have a lot of catching up to do."

A movement across the room caught Victoria's attention, and her gaze went to David, who had taken up residence against a wall. Apparently he'd chosen to stay in the background as she talked with Imogene.

What was he thinking? For years he'd thought, as she had, that she was a street kid, a misfit. But she wasn't. She was a Danforth. She had a home. A loving family. She was rich, for goodness sake!

"Have you met David?" she asked Imogene and Raf. Victoria held out her hand and he came to her side.

David took her hand and leaned close to her face. "Hey, you gave me a scare," he whispered.

"I'm sorry." Victoria didn't know what else to say. How did David feel about her now that he knew her real identity? She scoffed silently at herself. Who was she trying to fool? Why would who she was change how he felt about her? While their relationship had become intimate, he hadn't confessed his feelings went any deeper than lust. Her gaze swept over him again. His expression gave her little clue as to his thoughts.

"We talked while we were waiting for the doctor to examine you," Imogene replied. "David told us that you'd lived with his father until just a while ago. I know you lost him recently. I'm very sorry, honey," she said quietly, stroking her sister's arm.

At the thought of Edward, Victoria began crying again. She swallowed hard, forcing the tears back down. "David's father, Edward, was wonderful to me." Despite how David and his father had gotten along, she couldn't discount her own feelings for Edward. "He offered me a job and a place to live, gave me a future to look forward to." She didn't mention David's difficult relationship with his father. "He was a wonderful man who gave me the security I needed when I had nothing."

"That was very kind of him. I wish he were here for us to thank." She looked at David. "Please know how grateful our family is."

David nodded, but said nothing.

Sniffling, Victoria asked, "How is everyone? How are Mom and Dad? Are they okay?" Five years. She'd lost five years of her life. How did someone make up for that? But it didn't really matter, did it? She was back where she belonged now.

Or was she? She felt oddly misplaced. Though she had a life to return to, it would feel strange leaving the one she'd become accustomed to.

"They're on the way here," Imogene replied, breaking into her thoughts.

"I can't wait to see them. Do they know that I'm all right?"

Imogene brushed her hand across Victoria's cheek. "They do, honey, and so does the entire family by now, I'm quite sure."

"Tell me about them," she implored, wanting to hear everything she'd missed.

Imogene did her best, filling Victoria in on everything that had been happening with her siblings and cousins, about Jake, her oldest brother, and his wife Larissa.

"They have a three-year-old son." At Victoria's surprised expression, she added, "It's a long story, but he went to college with her and never knew she'd had his baby. But they're happily married now. They can't wait until we bring you home."

"What about Toby?" she asked, wondering about her other brother.

Her sister shook her head. "That's a long story, too. He's married. His wife's name is Heather and they also have a son."

"Oh, my gosh. I've missed so much," Victoria exclaimed with despair.

Imogene lightly touched her sister's hand. "Tori, I want you to know that we've never stopped searching for you. Mom and Dad, all of us, wouldn't give up hope that we'd find you one day." She started to cry again, this time more earnestly. "What happened, well, it was my fault, and I'm so sorry."

Crying along with her sister, Victoria grabbed tissues from the bedside table, gave her sister some, then dabbed at her own eyes. "Your fault? How?"

"I should have been there with you. Jake only gave you the tickets to that concert because he thought I was going with you. If I had, this would never have happened." She broke down, and Raf drew her to him, let her cry on his shoulder. When she garnered her strength, she looked at her sister. "Please forgive me."

"There's nothing to forgive, Genie. This wasn't your fault at all. It was mine. I was the one who invited Tanya." The memory was now so vivid in her mind, as if it were only yesterday. "I hadn't known her for very long, but she'd seemed as if she needed a friend."

Imogene gave a half laugh. "You always had such a big

heart." She looked at David. "She always wanted to take care of everyone. If any of us were sick, Tori made it her job to be at our beck and call, nursing us back to health."

"Well, this time it caught up with me. After the concert, Tanya and I headed to the car. I didn't know it, but she had planned to run away afterwards with her boyfriend. He was waiting for her outside the concert hall. She wanted me to give them a ride to a bus station. Though I felt uneasy about it, I told her I would." She endured her sister's tolerant expression. "I didn't know that they'd planned to steal my car."

"Oh, my God!" Imogene gasped.

"As we were riding, Tanya's boyfriend asked me to stop at a convenience store. I didn't want to, but he was acting a little weird, like he was on drugs or something, so I did. When we went to get back into the car, he took my keys and forced me to get into the back seat. That's when I realized that I was in real trouble. He took a route off the highway. After several turns, I lost track of where we were. Eventually, I decided I wasn't going to just sit there and let them get away with it, so I started arguing with him and hitting him from the back seat."

"He got really angry and stopped the car and told me get out. When I refused, he dragged me out of it." She blinked, then frowned as the memory of that awful night came back with clarity. "I stumbled and fell, and that's the last thing I remember."

David picked up her story from there. "The doctors who examined her said she had a concussion. They weren't sure how it happened." He looked at Tanya. "It must have been when you fell."

She nodded. "I guess they just left me there." Frowning, she asked, "But couldn't you have found all that out from Tanya?" Surely by now they would have questioned the girl.

Imogene shook her head. "No, honey. We've had an investigator searching for you, but neither he nor the police could even find your car. It was like you dropped off the face of the earth. The only information he could turn up was that Tanya Winters had gone into a group home. He was told that she had amnesia." Her eyes widened. "That must have been you!" she realized. "He tried to find her after that, to check out the story and see if she remembered anything, but the courts had lost her paperwork. Oh, my," she said, turning to Raf, "he was on the right trail all along, we just didn't know they thought *you* were Tanya."

"When the police found Victoria, she had Tanya's identification on her." David told them. He shook his head. "So it was Tanya who disappeared."

Victoria eyes widened. "That's why they thought I was Tanya. For the fun of it, we'd dyed our hair red and switched clothing." She laughed bitterly. "Well, I learned a hard lesson. Mom told me she didn't want me dressing like Tanya when we went to the concert. I should have listened to her."

Exhausted, she lay her head back on the bed and fought back a yawn. David studied her, then met Imogene's gaze across the bed. "Would you mind giving us a few minutes alone?"

"Of course," Imogene replied softly. "We'll be right outside if you need anything," she told her sister.

David waited until the door closed behind them, then because he couldn't stop himself, he leaned down and briefly kissed Victoria. Not wanting to unnerve her, he drew back and let his gaze drift over her face. She looked tired, but otherwise was as beautiful as always. "How are you really feeling?" he asked as he took her hand in his.

"Overwhelmed," she admitted, and now that she'd heard about her family, even more so. Victoria drew in a deep breath, then let it out slowly, her heartbeat quickening. "I can't believe all that's happened," she said, still tasting him on her lips, wishing his kiss meant more than just concern. "I remember everything now, but it's hard trying to sort it all out." Her throat felt swollen, and she took a cup of water from the table beside the bed. After taking a swallow, she put it down. "One minute I'm Tanya, and the next, I'm Victoria Danforth. I don't know what to think."

David stroked her forehead with the palm of his hand. "The doctor said you might be confused for a while, and for you to take it easy for the next few days. You've been through a lot, not just in the last few hours, but for the past five years. Don't try to sort it all out right away."

Pulling her hand away from his, she sat up again. "I can't help it. It all seems so surreal. I want to know everything, but it gets jumbled in my mind. And I can't help feeling that I've missed so much. I feel like there's two people inside me." She trembled. "It's scary."

David stroked her back. "Tori, I'm not going to let anything happen to you. I promise."

Victoria's gaze connected with his. *Tori.* Her name sounded strange on his lips. "Tori," she repeated. It even sounded a little strange coming from her.

He gave her a resolute look. "I have to call you something other than Tanya. Victoria is a beautiful name, but it doesn't feel, I don't know, right to me." For what they'd been through together, for what they'd shared, he wanted to say. But he didn't. He let her digest his words, then asked, "Do you mind if I call you Tori?"

"Tori is...nice."

"I mean it, you know," he said, his tone serious. "I don't want you to feel threatened in any way. I'm not going to let anyone hurt you."

Victoria wanted to believe him, wanted to believe that he would take care of her forever. Because he *wanted* to, not because he'd promised his father. But she just wasn't sure of anything anymore. Her two worlds had collided, and her life as she knew it had forever changed. Soon her family would be arriving, and surely they were expecting her to return to Savannah with them.

And she wanted to go. She wanted to see her brothers and their wives and children, wanted to catch up on every detail of their lives that she'd missed. Victoria had thought that she'd be happy living at Cottonwood for the rest of her life, but did she even belong there now?

Sadly, she had to face the truth. There was no permanent place for her in David's life. He'd never intimated there would be anything permanent between them. No, as much as it hurt to admit it, she belonged in Savannah with her family. Before all this occurred, she had been planning on leaving because she couldn't stay without his love.

Nothing had changed in their relationship.

Summoning all of her courage, she said, "I'm not your responsibility anymore, David." Her words seemed peculiar to her own ears. David had made a deathbed promise to his father that he'd take care of her, one that he'd told her he would keep.

She remembered back when he'd first arrived home. He'd been ready to ship her off to college to get her out of his life. Maybe he was more comfortable with her now because they'd had a sexual relationship, but that didn't mean he felt anything in his heart for her. Becoming lovers had only complicated things between them, because she'd fallen in love with him.

But David didn't love her.

He had no plans to stay on the plantation any longer than he had to. She'd heard that straight from his own mouth when she'd overheard his conversation with Justin. His life was in Atlanta. She'd known that before her memory had returned. Her memory returning merely facilitated a decision she'd already made.

And had provided a place for her to go. Home to Savannah.

David grimaced at her choice of words. "We've gone way beyond that, haven't we?"

"Because we were lovers?" she asked with surprising calm.

His gaze hardened. *Were lovers.* Not, because we *are* lovers. She was already thinking of the time they'd spent together in the past tense. He studied her, and suddenly an odd feeling of doom settled in his chest. He was losing her. He had found everything he'd ever wanted in this woman, but he hadn't seen it in time. Now she didn't need him.

The feeling of dread deepened. "I love you." She looked away and desperation set in. "I do," he said fiercely. He touched her face with the palm of his hand, turning her face to him and lifting her chin, willing her to look at him. "Tori, I—"

"Don't," she pleaded, and freed herself from him. "Don't do this, David. Not now." She pressed her lips together, wishing with all her heart that David's words of love were coming from his heart. But she knew better. When she'd been Tanya, she hadn't fit into his world. Now he thought because she was Victoria Danforth, an heiress, she did. All along she'd wished he was falling in love with her. Why hadn't he admitted his feelings when he thought she was a poor girl from the streets? Why now?

Did he truly love her?

Maybe he was telling himself that he did, but she wasn't going to be foolish enough to believe him. As much as it caused her pain to do so, she said, "I'm sorry, David. Everything has changed now. All this," she said, waving her arms around, then dropping them to her sides, "learning who I am, finding out what happened, it's all just too much. I think it would be best if you took me back to the plantation so that I can pack my things. I'd like to be ready to leave with my parents when they arrive."

David stepped back from her, stunned by her request. "You can't mean that. You belong at the plantation." Frustration built up inside him. He couldn't believe she was telling him she wanted to leave.

"The plantation," she whispered, and sighed at the realization. "That's what you wanted all along, isn't it? Cottonwood?"

David couldn't deny it, but he wanted so much more now. He wanted Victoria. He swallowed hard. "Yes, I did, but—"

"It's yours," she told him, her voice void of emotion. "The terms of the will stated that I could stay for as long as I wanted. If I leave, the plantation is yours, free and clear." She took a breath. "So now you'll have what you always wanted. Your family's plantation and me out of your life."

His lips twisted wryly. "You think that's what I want? The damn plantation?"

Instead of answering, she said quietly, "I'd like to get dressed now, please. Would you mind asking Genie to come back inside to help me?"

"Tori—"

"Please." Staring at him, she willed him to let her go. She'd already lost her heart to him. She wanted to leave with at least her self-respect. "I can't stay, David."

Not with doubt in her heart.

Because she'd never really know if he loved her for herself.

Twelve

David sat at the desk in his father's study, his heart aching. He couldn't believe that Victoria could just walk away from the plantation.

From him.

He'd told her he loved her, but it hadn't mattered. She had her old life back now. She was from a wealthy family, a family who loved her and wanted her home with them.

Everything had changed once she became aware of her true identity.

He leaned over, his head braced against his hands, wracking his brain for what he could do to change her mind. Until today, the only sure thing in her life had been Cottonwood. David would have bet his life that nothing could get her to leave.

But he had never planned on this. Victoria was an

heiress. She could do anything she wanted, live any-where she wanted.

She didn't need the plantation.

She didn't need him.

David had only himself to blame. Like a fool, he'd chosen the worst possible moment to bare his soul to her. She'd had the biggest shock of her life, and be-cause he was afraid of losing her, he'd confessed that he loved her.

No wonder she hadn't believed him. It sounded con-trived to his own ears.

She thought that he only wanted the plantation, and if he were honest with himself, he did. Coming home had been cathartic for him. He'd learned that he cared about Cottonwood, and he wanted it to continue to be successful—for his father.

At that realization, something shifted in his heart. The bitter feelings he'd held against his father for so long had vanished. Victoria was responsible for that. After his breakup with Melanie, David had thought that he'd never trust another woman again. But Victoria had scaled the barriers of his heart. Through her, he'd seen another side of his cold-hearted father. She'd taught him that in order to get on with his life, he had to let his harsh feelings for his father go.

Standing, David paced to the window. From the first, Edward had known there was something special about Victoria. David wasn't sure why. He would never know. But that's why his father had taken her in, why he had encouraged her. Trusted her with the operation of the plantation in his son's absence.

It was why he'd asked David to take care of her.

Somehow, his father had known that Victoria would

need him. He suspected, also, that Edward knew that he needed Victoria just as much.

But Victoria didn't know that, because David, trying to protect his heart, hadn't told her how he truly felt about her. Well, he wasn't going to let her go without a fight.

He loved her. With all his heart. God, she had to believe him.

He'd tried to talk to her again when they'd arrived back at Cottonwood, but Imogene had snatched her sister away to reminisce and bring her up-to-date on family matters. David hadn't wanted to get in the way, so he'd gone into his office. But he couldn't let Victoria leave without talking to her one more time.

He couldn't live without her.

Victoria stared out the window of her bedroom at the plantation. In only moments, her parents would arrive. As much as she wanted to see them, she dreaded every minute that ticked by. Each one inched her closer and closer to the moment when she'd have to leave David.

After her release papers had been signed by the doctor, she'd dressed and they'd left the hospital. By the time she checked out, the news media had staked out the entire area. The hospital staff had ushered her out through a private exit in order to avoid the horde of reporters who had set up camp just outside the front doors of the building. She knew that eventually she'd have to talk to the media, but she just couldn't do it now. Not while all of her emotions were on edge. She needed time to adjust to all that had happened to her.

Time to get over leaving David.

She fought back the tears that threatened. Imogene had reached their parents on their cell phone, giving them directions to the plantation and again assuring them that Victoria was all right.

All right.

Shivering, Victoria faced the truth. She was never going to feel all right again because she was leaving her heart here.

With David.

"Nothing will be the same when you go back."

At the sound of David's voice, Victoria's heart stilled. She turned, and her gaze found his. He stood in the frame of the doorway, a looming presence, his expression serious and intense, and oh, God, he could melt her with just a look. How was she ever going to get over him?

"Savannah?" A wistful look flashed through her eyes. "No, I suppose not. I'm sure it's changed."

"I'm not talking about Savannah." Shoving away from the door, David ambled across the room, stopping only inches from her. "*You've* changed. You're not the same girl you were when you left."

That was true, she thought. Now she was a woman, and she knew how it felt to be loved by him. "I suppose I have. But Savannah is my home."

"You're wrong, Tori. This is your home."

"No." Tears brimmed in her eyes as she shook her head. "Cottonwood is yours, not mine, David. It always has been."

He touched her face with the palm of his hand. "At one time I thought that was true," he admitted, shrugging his shoulders. "When I came back, I was ready to run you off."

"I know," she said quietly. "I was never after Cottonwood, or your father's money."

David let out a breath. "I didn't really think you were."

"You didn't?" Her eyebrows lifted.

"I was trying get rid of you because I was so damned attracted to you and I didn't want to be."

Caught off-guard by his confession, Tori stared at him, disbelief written on her features.

"Does that surprise you, Tori? That I wanted you?"

He moved closer and she felt engulfed by his male scent. It wrapped around her like a warm blanket, pulling her to him. "Yes," she whispered, wanting to believe him. But David had the power to destroy her.

"I've wanted you ever since I walked back into this house. Actually, I've wanted you for years. While I was living in Atlanta, I thought about coming back for you, but I couldn't risk the wrath of my father so I stayed away."

Victoria searched his face. His eyes were steady, his expression solemn. He was telling the truth. "I had no idea." At least, she'd had no idea when he'd left five years ago that he'd wanted her. Now, though, she did. But desire wasn't the same as love. As much as it hurt, she still couldn't stay here—not without his love.

"I didn't want you to know how I felt about you. To be honest, I'd been hurt, first by my father and then by Melanie. I didn't think I could ever trust someone again."

"But you can now?"

"You're unlike any woman I've ever met, Tori. You showed me how to let my bitterness for my father go. You taught me to forgive him."

Licking her lips, Victoria stared at him. "He loved you in his own way."

"I know that now," he said. "Just like I know that I can trust you with my heart."

"Really, David?"

"You taught me something else. You taught me how to love again."

Hope filled Victoria. She wanted so much to believe him. "I want to believe you," she whispered.

"I love you, Tori. Please don't leave me."

The heat of his body drew her toward him. Her heart hammering, she lifted her hands to his face. "You love me?" she asked, a shiver going through her.

Looking into her eyes, David slipped his arms around her. He leaned his head down and touched his lips to hers. Then he straightened, keeping her within the circle of his arms. "I do, sweetheart. And I want to spend the rest of my life showing you how much you mean to me."

Victoria's eyes teared. "Oh, David, I love you, too. I have for so long." She slipped her arms around his waist.

He groaned. "I've waited a long time for you." David felt the tension leave his body as she held him. His lips took hers in a heated kiss, his tongue briefly exploring her mouth before he raised his head. "I thought I was too late. I thought you were going to leave me," he admitted.

She smiled up at him. "I was. I didn't think you meant it when you told me at the hospital that you loved me."

He kissed her again. "I picked a heck of a time to admit how I felt about you, waiting until you'd gotten your memory back. But when Imogene confronted you at the Thanksgiving celebration, and it became clear that you were really her sister, I realized I could lose you. I've been such a fool. I should have told you a long time ago that I was in love with you. When you got your memory back, I could see you slipping away from my life. I began to panic."

She leaned up and kissed his mouth. "It was quite a shock learning my identity."

"For both of us." David tightened his arms around

her. "I know that you want to be with your family now. Though I want to keep Cottonwood, I'm willing to move to Savannah so that I can be with you."

Her eyes widened as she leaned away to get a better look at his face. "You'd move to Savannah? What about your plans to return to Atlanta?"

"I'm not going back to Atlanta," he told her.

"But I heard you. Yesterday. You were on the phone with Justin, and I heard you tell him that your plans hadn't changed. I assumed you meant that you were planning on returning to Atlanta when the term of the will was up."

Understanding dawned on David. "That's why you suddenly become so quiet and distant, why you wanted to return to Cottonwood so quickly?"

She licked her lips. "Well, yes."

"Sweetheart, that conversation had nothing to do with you, with us. It was about business."

"Really?"

"Believe me, honey, the only plan I have is to live with you wherever you want."

"Oh, David, I love you so much." Victoria smiled. In all of her dreams, she'd never thought that her life would turn out like this. She'd arrived at Cottonwood alone and confused, her memory wiped from her mind.

From the moment she'd seen David, he'd stolen her heart. Now she had her memory, her family and David's love. It was a fairy tale come true.

"What about your company in Atlanta?"

"I've turned the day-to-day operations over to Justin. He's more than capable of running the company. Once you've had time to get reacquainted with your family, I'd like to come back here, make it our home."

Victoria's heart flipped. "Live here?" she breathed out, her pulse racing. "At Cottonwood?"

"I've learned a lot since I came back home. I've accepted that my father couldn't change who he was."

"I think it broke his heart when your mother died. He never recovered. But he loved you, David. Like you, he didn't want to trust his heart to anyone, not even his child."

"I know. I'm sorry that we didn't totally iron out our differences before he died, but I believe we made a peace, of sorts."

"You did," she replied, pleased by his insight. But that didn't pacify her uneasiness about his being happy here. Finding acceptance of your past and living in your ancestral home were two different things. The last thing she'd ever want is for him to regret such a choice. "And you're sure you wouldn't mind living here?"

"I fell in love with you here, Tori. I want to live here with you for the rest of my life." David took her hand and knelt down on the floor on one knee. "I love you. Will you marry me?"

Delighted, she stared incredulously at him. "Oh, yes, yes!" She hugged him. Leaning away she looked into his eyes, as a wondrous thought hit her. "Only—"

He eyed her with speculation. "Only what?"

She grinned. "This is an awfully big house. How would you feel about filling it with children?"

With a laugh, he kissed her hungrily. "I think we should get started on it right away. How do you feel about short engagements?"

Epilogue

Dressed in a stunning white strapless gown, Victoria made her way through the crowd of people gathered in the grand ballroom of one of the finest hotels in Savannah. The celebration of her Uncle Abraham's election to the Senate was in full swing. Continuous chatter from the crowd blended with the sounds of big band music.

After her parents had arrived at the plantation, she'd spent some time alone with them, assuring them that she was fine. Being with them had been wonderful. Once everything had calmed down, she and David informed them of their plans to be married. They'd already told Imogene and Raf. Imogene had confessed that she'd suspected there was something romantic between them.

It had gone well, she thought, as she pushed open the door of the ladies' room. Her parents had responded with enthusiasm, easily accepting their adult daughter's decision. After spending time with David, they seemed to be crazy about him, which thrilled her all the more. Over the past few days, he had been welcomed into the fold of the Danforth family.

So that she could visit with her entire family, Victoria had returned to Savannah for a few days. David had come with her, and they had spent hours visiting with her siblings, aunts, uncles and many cousins. All of them had been supportive and loving, and Victoria felt like the luckiest woman on earth.

But it only took a few days of being away from the plantation before she began missing her home. She and David had eventually returned to enjoy the peace and quite of the country.

Or so they thought.

She thought back over the past week. The media frenzy had been totally exhausting, and their telephone hadn't stopped ringing. Her name and picture had been plastered on practically every newspaper in the country, as well as shown on all the major television networks. Reporters had been camping out at the entrance to their property for days.

Victoria had held a press conference just yesterday to talk to the reporters about her ordeal. Still, that did not satisfy their thirst for information. Their telephone had continued to ring.

David had insisted on hiring someone to represent them who could field requests for interviews. It was then that they'd decided on a course of action that would, indeed, surprise her family when they broke the news to them tonight.

Making her way out of a stall, Victoria began washing her hands. She was just about finished when she

heard someone else come into the ladies' room. Looking up, she saw Nicola Granville, her uncle's campaign
manager.

"Hello, Nicola," she said, smiling at the beautiful
red-haired woman she'd met earlier in the evening.

"Victoria!" Startled, she stopped in her tracks. "How
are you?"

"I'm fine. Thanks for asking."

"We haven't had a chance to talk. I want you to know
that I'm glad you're back with your family."

Victoria gave Nicola a warm smile. "Thanks. I hope
my reappearance hasn't caused adverse publicity for
my uncle."

"Hardly," Nicola replied. "He's been joking that it
had gotten him the sympathy vote." She chuckled. "Seriously, Abraham is thrilled that you're back home, safe
and sound. All of your family is. They can't stop talking about it." Suddenly, she stopped speaking and put
her hand to her forehead.

"Are you all right?" Victoria asked, noticing the
woman's pale complexion.

Nicola replied, "Yes, I'm fine."

But clearly she wasn't. Victoria walked toward her
as she dried her hands with a paper towel. Before she
could say anything more, Nicola cupped her hand over
her mouth, then darted around her. She pushed through
the door of a stall and abruptly lost the contents of her
stomach in the toilet.

Victoria rushed to help her. "Oh, honey," she cried.
"You are certainly not all right." She darted to the paper
towel dispenser, grabbed a few towels, then ran them
under cool water. Returning to Nicola's side, she held the
compress against her forehead until she felt a little better.

"Thank you," Nicola said sincerely. She walked to the sink, rinsed out her mouth and washed her hands.

"Maybe you should sit down for a few moments," Victoria suggested. She spotted some tissues on the vanity. Snatching some, she gave them to Nicola.

Nicola, looking as weak as an injured bird, shook her head. "I feel better now."

"Really?" Victoria asked. She found that hard to believe. The woman's skin looked clammy, and her skin tone had regained none of its color.

The other woman shrugged. "I'm sure I am. I must have some kind of twenty-four-hour bug or something."

Victoria frowned. "Really? Well, I hope that's all it is. I heard the flu is going around." She tossed a paper towel into the trash can. "Is there anything else I can do for you?"

"No, I'm fine. But thank you."

"Well, if you think you're okay, I guess I'll go."

"I'll be all right," Nicola insisted. "Thanks again for helping me."

"You're welcome. I'll see you later," Victoria answered. She left the bathroom and went in search of David.

"Looking for me?" David asked, slipping his arm around her as she walked back into the ballroom. He nuzzled her neck, and she moved into his embrace.

"Always," she murmured, her eyes shining as she gazed at him.

"Are you all right?" he asked. She continued to amaze him. Intelligent and graceful, she'd handled everything that had been thrown at her with innate charm. She'd had the reporters eating out of her hand.

"I'm wonderful." Pressing her mouth to his, she moaned softly when he drew away. "Are you ready?"

"I have to admit that I'm having second thoughts." Although David had never shied away from confrontation, he wasn't sure he was ready to face Victoria's family.

"Oh, you can't back out now, darling," she said, then started leading the way to the table where her parents and the rest of her family were seated. "It's too late."

"You're right," he agreed as he followed her across the room. "But they're going to be shocked."

Victoria smiled back at him. "Not as shocked as they were when Genie called them and told them she'd found me."

They arrived at the table where Miranda and Harold were seated along with Imogene, Raf, Jake and his wife, Larissa. Toby and Heather had left earlier in the day to return to Wyoming. Instead of sitting down, Victoria and David continued to stand beside the table. "Mom, Dad, everyone," Victoria stated to get their attention.

Everyone stopped speaking and looked at her. Victoria smiled at David, then shifted her gaze to her family. "David and I have an announcement."

Jake winked at his sister. "If you're going to tell us that you're going to another concert, the answer is no."

"Very cute." Everyone burst out laughing. Victoria gave her brother a mock look of frustration. She'd endured a lot of teasing since she'd returned, but she knew her brothers loved her, and it made her feel even more endeared to them. "No," she said patiently, a smile playing on her lips, "that's not what I'm going to say."

Taking a deep breath, she licked her lips. "There's no easy way to say this so I'm just going to tell you straight out. David and I eloped today. We're married!" Beaming, she held out her hand and showed them her rings, a gold band with diamonds that matched the round brilliant diamond he'd given her the day after he'd asked her to marry him.

"Married?" Harold exclaimed.

Miranda got to her feet. "What?" In moments, everyone was standing and talking at once.

"We know you're surprised, and probably even disappointed," David said. "But we decided against having a wedding, and we didn't want to wait to pledge our commitment to each other."

"This past week has been crazy," Victoria explained breathlessly. "The media hasn't left us alone. We figured it would be months before the publicity would settle down and we could get married without nationwide attention focused on us."

David spoke directly to Miranda and Harold. "I want you all to know that I love your daughter. She's the most important thing in my life."

Though tears dotted her cheeks, Miranda smiled. "I can't say that I'm not sorry we missed the wedding, but we understand. With Abraham's election to the Senate, and finding my daughter, the reporters haven't left us alone, either." She came around the table and embraced Victoria. "Congratulations, Tori. I'm so happy for you. You've chosen well."

Harold hugged his daughter next, then shook his new son-in-law's hand. "Welcome to our family," he said, and his eyes weren't dry. "Take care of her."

David nodded. "You have my word."

Soon everyone was hugging the new bride and groom, wishing them the best. When the band began playing a waltz, David grasped Victoria's hand. "Dance with me?"

She smiled, her eyes shining. "Love to."

He led her to the dance floor, then pulled her against him. She slid her arms around his neck and looked up at him. "That wasn't so bad, was it?"

"Your parents are wonderful. I'm not sure I would have reacted the same way if I'd been in their shoes."

"They love me," she said simply.

"I love you, Tori. With all my heart."

Victoria's arms tightened around him. "I love you, too." She pressed closer to him, then urged his mouth to hers. David's tongue made a foray into her mouth, touching hers, making Victoria moan with desire. "I've got a great idea," she whispered against his mouth.

He licked his lips, tasting her. "I'm listening," he answered, wishing they weren't in the middle of a crowded dance floor. He wanted to be alone with his wife.

"I don't think anyone would really miss us if we left." Her eyes softened with desire, and she moved against him suggestively. "Let's slip out of here. I want to go home. I can think of a better way for us to spend the rest of this evening."

"I like the way you think," David answered. After a lingering kiss, he led her off the dance floor.

Slipping by their table, she discreetly grabbed her purse. Without anyone noticing, Victoria and David escaped into the night. A full moon illuminated their way as they drove toward home.

Victoria sat close to her husband, her arm around his. Content, she rested her head on his shoulder. Only a few weeks ago, she'd been all alone in the world. Now she knew her true identity, and the emptiness that had been inside her had been filled with her family's love and caring.

And David's love.

Her heart swelled. She'd loved him from the moment

she'd seen him, and she was going to love him for the rest of her life. She smiled dreamily at him, and he leaned over and kissed her. Victoria deepened the kiss, drawing his tongue into her mouth.

Groaning, David broke off their kiss. "Behave. I'm about ready to pull this car over."

"That sounds engaging," Victoria replied.

"Don't tempt me. I want to take you home where I can make love to you in bed. I'd hate to tell our son that he was conceived in the back of a car."

Victoria grinned. "Our son?"

David chuckled. "Or daughter." He squeezed her hand. "I never dreamed that I'd be lucky enough to be married to you, let alone become a father to our children."

"I'm the lucky one," she whispered.

And she was. Enchanted, Victoria snuggled against him, anxious to begin the rest of their lives together.

* * * * *

Look for the thrilling conclusion to
DYNASTIES: THE DANFORTHS
next month with
SHOCKING THE SENATOR
by Leanne Banks.

Silhouette® Desire®

Coming in December 2004

**The Scent of Lavender
series continues with**

Jennifer Greene's

WILD IN THE MOMENT

(Silhouette Desire #1622)

The whirring blizzard, the cracking fire and their
intimate quarters had Daisy Campbell and
Teague Larson unexpectedly sharing a wild
moment. The two hardly seemed like a match
made in heaven…so why couldn't Daisy turn
down Teague's surprise business deal and
many more wild moments?

The Scent of Lavender

The Campbell sisters awaken to passion
when love blooms where they least expect it!

Available at your favorite retail outlet.

passionate powerful provocative love stories

**Silhouette Desire delivers
strong heroes, spirited heroines
and compelling love stories.**

Desire features your favorite authors,
including

Annette Broadrick,
Ann Major,
Anne McAllister
and Cait London.

**Passionate, powerful and provocative
romances *guaranteed!***

For superlative authors, sensual stories
and sexy heroes, choose Silhouette Desire.

passionate powerful provocative love stories

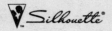

INTIMATE MOMENTS™

and

Linda Winstead Jones

present

**When your back's against the wall
and your heart's on the line...**

Running Scared

(Intimate Moments #1334)

In the jungles of South America, Quinn Calhoun
must rescue impetuous Olivia Larkin from the
dangerous hurricane of corruption, kidnappings and
murder that whirls around her. But protecting her
means spending time in *very* close quarters....

Available December 2004 at your favorite retail outlet.

And look for the next LAST CHANCE HEROES title,
Truly, Madly, Dangerously (IM #1348), in February 2005.

COMING NEXT MONTH

#1621 SHOCKING THE SENATOR—Leanne Banks
Dynasties: The Danforths
Abraham Danforth had tried to deny his attraction to his campaign manager, Nicola Granville, for months—although they *had* shared a secret night of passion. With the election won and Abraham becoming Georgia's new senator, would the child Nicola now carried become the scandal that would ruin his career?

#1622 WILD IN THE MOMENT—Jennifer Greene
The Scent of Lavender
The whirring blizzard, the cracking fire and their intimate quarters had Daisy Campbell and Teague Larson unexpectedly sharing a wild moment. The two hardly seemed like a match made in heaven...so why couldn't Daisy turn down Teague's surprise business deal and *many more* wild moments?

#1623 THE ICE MAIDEN'S SHEIKH—Alexandra Sellers
Sons of the Desert
Beauty Jalia Shahbazi had been a princess-under-wraps for twenty-seven years and that was how she planned to keep it. That was until sexy Sheikh Latif Al Razzaqi Shahin awakened her Middle Eastern roots... and her passion. But Latif wanted to lay claim to more than Jalia's body— and she dared not offer more.

#1624 FORBIDDEN PASSION—Emilie Rose
Lynn Riggan's brother-in-law Sawyer was everything her recently deceased husband was not: caring, giving and loving. The last thing Lynn was looking for was forbidden passion, but after briefly giving in to their intense mutual attraction, she couldn't get Sawyer out of her head... or her heart. Might an unexpected arrival give her all she'd ever wanted?

#1625 RIDING THE STORM—Brenda Jackson
Jayla Coles had met many Mr. Wrongs when she finally settled on visiting the sperm bank to get what she wanted. Then she met the perfect storm— fire captain Storm Westmoreland. They planned on a no-strings-attached affair, but their brief encounter left them with more than just lasting memories....

#1626 THE SEDUCTION REQUEST—Michelle Celmer
Millionaire restaurateur Matt Conway returned to his hometown to prove he'd attained ultimate success. But when he ran into former best friend and lover, Emily Douglas, winning over her affection became his number-one priority. Problem was, she was planning on marrying another man...and Matt was just the guy to make her change her mind.

SDCNM1104